O9-BTI-459

Simeon's Fire

Cathryn Clinton

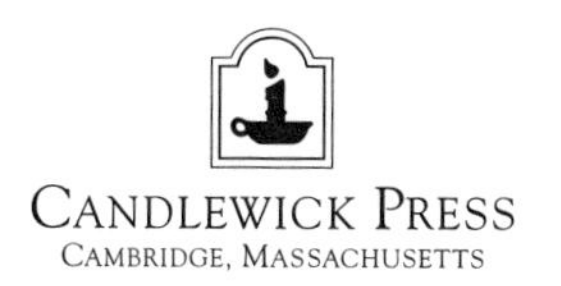

CANDLEWICK PRESS
CAMBRIDGE, MASSACHUSETTS

This is a work of fiction. Names, characters, places, and incidents are either products of the author's imagination or, if real, are used fictitiously.

First edition 2005

Library of Congress Cataloging-in-Publication Data is available.

Library of Congress Catalog Card Number 2005051208

ISBN 0-7636-2707-0

2 4 6 8 10 9 7 5 3 1

Printed in the United States of America

This book was typeset in Granjon.

Candlewick Press
2067 Massachusetts Avenue
Cambridge, Massachusetts 02140

visit us at www.candlewick.com

This book is dedicated to The Truth, Jesus Christ,
and to my husband, Dan, who knows
what a good father would say.

Chapter 1

Simeon Zook listened to the quiet in the house. He was awake before everyone. Even *Daat* and *Maam* were still asleep.

Simeon heard things that others missed because he listened more than he talked. Or that's what his *Grossmudder* said. Simeon's ears were tuned to the sounds of the farm: birds, animals, the old barn, and the weather. He felt the sounds deep inside him. He knew when things were right and wrong.

As he lay there in bed, he heard the *seet-seet* of the chickadee and the slurred whistle of a cardinal. The cardinal nested in the spirea bush under his window. He felt a prickle inside and sat up. He would check on Lena A, his cow.

Simeon slipped his legs over the side of the double bed that he and Little Elam shared, and stepped down on the wide warped floorboard that was right by his bed. It squeaked. In his hurry he'd forgotten about it, but Little Elam didn't move.

Sylvan, their eldest brother, shifted, but he soon fell back into a snore. Jonas, his other brother, had his head under the pillow and hadn't heard a thing. None of his brothers would want to be up early. Five o'clock chores were early enough.

Simeon started dressing. He put on his teal shirt and pulled up his black broadfall pants and suspenders. He grabbed his flashlight, went downstairs and out the front door.

He was only two steps away from the porch when something wrapped itself around his leg, almost tripping him. It was Mouse, his favorite barn cat, with something for Simeon to see. Simeon moved his flashlight around until he caught sight of a little animal a foot away. It was a dead shrew. "*Ach,* Mouse, why do you catch the shrews? You don't like the smell of them, and you won't eat them! Stick with mousing." Simeon bent down and picked up Mouse. He stroked the cat as he walked toward the barn. Mouse rubbed his head against Simeon's chest. "I'll bring you a little treat after milking," Simeon said as he put Mouse down.

Simeon stood by the little stand of trees not too far from the house. He didn't hear any new bird sounds, only the mourning dove and the goldfinch. They were awake early today. He'd already written those two down in his bird journal this year.

Looking and listening for birds had started when he was four. He had been sitting in his *Grossmudder's* lap on the front porch when she'd pointed to a hummingbird by its feeder. "If you are very quiet and still, one may sit on your hand," she'd said. The hummingbird flew away at the sound of her words, but *Grossmudder* walked to the feeder, leaving Simeon in her rocker. She placed a little of the liquid on her hand, and then she held out her hand out and waited. The hummingbird came back to the feeder, and then it floated above her hand for the longest time. Simeon held his breath, and then with swift, quick darts it touched her palm. Simeon heard the tiny flutter of its wings.

"Simeon," *Grossmudder* said, "do you want to learn the birds?"

"Yes," Simeon answered.

"I believe you have a still place in your heart where you can already hear their sounds, *ya*?"

Simeon had nodded. "And soon you will know them with your eyes, too," she'd said.

No hummingbirds today, though. Simeon left the trees and walked to the big barn where they kept the milking cows and the horses and ponies. The small barn held the dry cows that weren't being milked, as well as the heifers that were too old to be fed like the calves but not old enough to give milk.

Simeon breathed deeply when he entered the big barn. He liked the tangy, cut-grass smell of the feed. It was strong, stronger than the smell of manure even. Simeon used his flashlight to find the stall where Lena A, his cow, was standing. Simeon reached over and scratched the little dip right behind her horns, and Lena A looked up and leaned her head toward him. *Daat* had said that he'd never seen a cow act like a pet, but trust Simeon to raise one. Everyone knew that Simeon was good with animals.

It was a tradition in the family to get a heifer for

your eighth birthday, because that's what they had done in *Daat*'s family when he was a boy. Lena, Simeon's oldest and only sister, had gotten her heifer the day before Simeon was born. She'd named her cow Arie, so that is also what she called Simeon. No one minded; since so many Amish have similar names, nicknaming is common.

Two years ago, Simeon had turned eight and gotten his heifer. He'd watched when the heifer was born and had given her the first little scratch on her head when she was only an hour old. He'd named her Lena A, which was short for Lena Arie, just to even things up with his sister, a name for a name.

Lena A was coming into her first calving. "How are you doing?" he said to the cow. It looked like her udder was fuller, or springing, as *Daat* said. "Is today the day? I'll be looking for a glazey look in your eyes."

Simeon listened to Lena A's chewing, breathing, and swishing. She stamped one hoof. Simeon rubbed her side. He kept his hand on her as he walked around her. He stilled himself until he couldn't hear his own thoughts. He tuned in to the deep place within him, the place where he just knew things. Something wasn't right. The prickly feeling that had brought him out here was growing into a gnawing. If things went wrong with a calving, the vet would have to be called. "I'll look after you," Simeon said. "I promise."

Simeon headed back to the house. When he got there, everyone was up and dressing.

Daat said, *"Gut Marye"*—good morning in *Deitsch,* the Amish dialect. "Checking on Lena A?" *Daat* pulled on the loose, straggly beard that reached his shirt and ducked his head in a quick nod, as he did nearly every time he talked.

"Ya," Simeon answered. "I think it will be soon, and I think there might be something wrong."

Maam had started on breakfast, and Lena was rolling out pie crusts. *Maam* turned from the gas stove and smiled at Simeon. "Knowing you, I'm sure you'll be minding her today."

Simeon nodded.

"I trust you to let me know how things are going. We'll call the vet if we need to," *Daat* said.

"Ya," Simeon answered.

Little Elam got the dog food to feed Ruff, the husky. Simeon headed back out to the big barn with Sylvan, Jonas, and *Daat.* He hurried to catch up to *Daat*'s long-legged, loose-armed stride. It didn't take long for Simeon to catch up because he was tall like his father. Even though he was only ten, Simeon was close in height to Sylvan, who was sixteen, and taller than Jonas, who was fourteen.

Simeon's brothers both took after the King side of the family. They had short legs, dark wiry hair, big heads, and wide faces. Their faces were alike too; they had turned-up noses, round chins with clefts in them, and small round deep-set eyes. Some people thought they were twins, but Jonas had a star-shaped scar on his face, and Sylvan had a space in his front teeth and a crooked little finger on his left hand that stuck out funny. There were lots of differences, if you looked for them. And Simeon did.

When he was little, Simeon had wished he looked like his older brothers, but he'd given up on that and settled for the long-legged, blond looks of his dad. He was going to be taller than both of his brothers anyway. And four-year-old Little Elam, who was named for his father, was looking more like Simeon every day, or so *Maam* said. Two boys for each side of the family seemed right to Simeon.

In the barn, *Daat* put the milkers together while Sylvan disinfected the teats of the cows. Jonas started shoveling the cow feed into the wheelbarrow. Simeon climbed up into the haymow to throw down a couple of bales of hay for the horses. He would feed the dry cows and heifers in the small barn after breakfast.

Simeon lit a lantern, raised it slowly, and hung it on the post. No barn fires here, he thought. They didn't have electric lights in the barn or in their house. Running electrical wires was a connection to the world, and staying separate from the ways of the world was important. *Daat* used power that he could take care of by himself: generators, battery power, bottled gas for the house, and windmills.

With a pitchfork, Simeon removed the old straw and pitched the new straw into every stall. The whine of the diesel engine that powered the milking units made a loud noise, almost drowning out Simeon's voice, so he raised it to call out to the horses, “Hey, you tractors! I’m bringing your gasoline.” It was his own little joke, because the Amish use farm horses instead of tractors. Using horses for farm work slows life down and keeps families working together.

Simeon called out to the horses, “Hey, Bud. Hey, Roger. You hungry this morning?” The Belgians looked toward Simeon as he gave them their oats and water. He patted Roy and Chip as he fed them. “Ready to work?” He asked. “What will it be, five acres or ten?” His dad would use them for some kind of work today. Simeon wondered what.

Bob kicked the side of the stall right before Simeon walked in. “Settle yourself,” Simeon said as he calmed the big horse. Bob stood seventeen hands and weighed one ton. Sylvan, who was five foot eight inches, had to stand on his tiptoes to see over Bob’s shoulder. Cap, Bob’s partner, just stood there.

As he fed the last of the workhorses, Butch and Mae, he said, “Here you are, you giants.” The two gray Percherons worked well together, but Mae was very old. She wasn’t keeping up. Her plowing days were just about over. Simeon patted her on his way out of their stall.

A song sparrow flew over Simeon's head as he walked to the ponies. It sat on a white wooden beam and sang. Simeon tried to whistle its song as he fed the ponies, then he lay down on a bale of hay and dozed a little when he was done. He heard *Daat's* voice as he, Sylvan, and Jonas walked toward the house. Simeon jumped up and followed them. They all headed inside for breakfast; Simeon sat down by Little Elam.

Daat said, "Put your heads down," which was the signal for silent prayer before breakfast. With his head down, Simeon saw Little Elam's leg wiggle. Simeon knew that Little Elam was peeking up at *Daat* to see when he'd move, so that Little Elam could grab the cereal box before Jonas did.

Simeon waited for the fried eggs, potatoes, and scrapple to be passed. He poured lots of syrup on the scrapple. He ate fast and belched loudly.

"What do you think we should do today?" *Daat* asked. He looked at Simeon and Jonas. Simeon knew that Sylvan, being oldest, had more farmwork experience. He probably already knew the answer.

"Hoe tobacco," said Simeon.

"Cut hay," said Jonas. "There was a red sky last night. And it's not too humid. Good haying weather."

Daat smiled. "Both are good ideas. We'll do both. The front that came through left us a beautiful day."

Daat turned to Little Elam. "You will feed the calves today." Little Elam smiled at Simeon. *Daat* continued, "And then you come ride with me as I cut hay." Simeon heard the smile in his father's voice. Simeon had learned to drive the horses by sitting on his father's lap, too.

"Sylvan, will you check the fence by the north pasture? Jonas, you help him, and the two of you can hoe tobacco this afternoon. If we don't have heavy dew, we'll rake the hay on Monday morning."

They had silent prayer again after breakfast, which was their custom, and then *Maam* and Lena cleared the table as the rest picked up their straw hats and headed outside.

Chapter 2

Simeon whisked the big straw hat off Jonas's head. It sailed out in the yard, and Jonas said, "Big hats for big brains," as he ran after it. Jonas's head was bigger than *Daat*'s.

Simeon said, "Flies have short legs and are soon tired."

Jonas yelled back as he headed into the barn, "It's not size of the legs, or a cow could catch a rabbit."

Simeon laughed and yelled, "Little Elam."

"Here," Little Elam answered right behind him.

Simeon jumped and said, "You could be my shadow, you are always so close." Little Elam grinned.

“I guess you’re ready, then,” Simeon said.

“For sure,” Little Elam answered. He stretched up to make himself look tall.

Simeon and Little Elam walked into the barn and filled the big bottle that was used to feed the calves. “Here, Little Elam, now you carry it out.” Little Elam carried the bottle. His steps were slow, careful. This was going to take a long time. Ruff walked beside them. They walked over to the little houses where the calves lived.

Little Elam had followed Simeon around while he was doing chores for the last year. So Simeon didn’t need to say anything as Little Elam fed the first calf.

“Be careful of the next one, Little Elam,” Simeon said. “He’s the stupidest one.” The calf was tugging hard at the bottle. “*Net so hatt*— not so hard,” Simeon said to the calf. “He pulls so hard, he spills half of it.” Simeon watched as Little Elam went back to the barn to fill the bottle again. He came out and fed another calf. “You are a hard worker,” Simeon said.

Simeon walked toward the smaller barn, calling over his shoulder, “Go ahead.” He went inside the small barn to feed the dry cows and heifers. When he was done, he came back out of the barn and saw that Little Elam was still working.

Simeon stood next to Little Elam as he fed the last calf. "Hey, wait," Simeon said. He took the big bottle from Little Elam's hands. He bent down and squirted it into a metal dish on the ground. "Don't forget Mouse," he said. "It's our secret." Simeon knew this secret had been passed down from *Daat* to Sylvan to Jonas to him, and now he was passing it on to Little Elam.

Little Elam smiled. He'd watched Simeon do this before, but Simeon had never let him in on the secret of it. And the secret was what made it special.

After taking the bottle back to the big barn, Little Elam said, "Simeon, I want to practice driving today. Will you hitch up the ponies for me?" Simeon started hitching them up to the little pony cart. While he did so, Little Elam called to Ruff, who ran over.

"Now you will take a nice ride," he said. "I need someone to ride with me." Ruff didn't move. "If you aren't getting in, then off with you," Little

Elam said. He sounded just like *Daat,* Simeon thought as he laughed quietly.

"Here, Little Elam. I've got an idea." Simeon was done with the hitching. "Climb up there and drive over to the calf houses." When they got to the calf houses, Simeon picked up the metal dish that held Mouse's secret milk and put it in the cart. He scooped up the two barn cats that had been lapping up the milk and put them in the back of the cart.

"Giddyap," Little Elam said. He yanked the reins, and the ponies jerked forward, pulling on Little Elam so that he almost fell out. The milk spilled all over the cart. The cats jumped out, and the ponies trotted right over to the barn door and stopped.

Simeon laughed and laughed.

Little Elam turned and looked at the cart. "Where are the cats?" he said.

"They jumped out a long time ago, and I think the ponies are still hungry," Simeon said when he caught his breath. "We'll have a driving lesson on another day." They cleaned up the cart and left it to dry in the sun.

"Why, Little Elam, you are quite the driver," *Maam* called from the doorway of the house. She stepped outside with a gallon jug of water in her hand. "Here, boys, take this out to the field with you. You'd better hurry along." She handed it to Simeon.

Joe-pye weed and Queen Anne's lace brushed their legs as they walked barefoot at the edge of the field. Two squirrels raced each other along the fence. "I think the little one will win," said Little Elam.

A crow dove at them, and Little Elam tightened his grip on Simeon's hand. "We are in his territory, Little Elam," Simeon said. "He was there yesterday. Just keep walking, and he will see that we are only passing through. Maybe a great horned owl is nearby, and the crow is heckling the owl to make sure it doesn't get the babies in her nest. I would do the same, wouldn't you?" Little Elam nodded.

When the boys got to *Daat,* he stopped the horses. He pulled out a big handkerchief and pulled off his straw hat. He wiped his face and then took a long, long drink of water. Little Elam climbed up on the seat with *Daat.* The mower was hooked up behind four of the horses. Daat drank a lot more of the water. Little Elam waved to Simeon as Simeon walked back to the house.

When Simeon went in for lunch, *Grossmudder* was there. She was a small, round woman. Her cape and apron were pulled in at the middle to give her a waist. Her black-stockinged ankles were thick. She had a bad hip, and she leaned to one side as she walked. Her hair had been pulled back tight for so many years that the part in the middle was nearly an inch wide.

Grossmudder usually dressed in black. Mourning was called for when a relative died, even a cousin, and at her age, someone was always dying. She lived in a little apartment that was built onto the back of the house. It was called the *Grossdawdi* house. *Grossdawdi* had lived there too, but he had died when Simeon was five.

"No new birds this morning," Simeon told her. *Grossmudder* nodded and said, "I listened to a mockingbird last night." The drag of her foot scraped the cracked linoleum as she placed a big pot of chicken potpie on the table. Lena put on bowls of coleslaw and applesauce. *Maam* put bread and strawberry jam on the table.

After lunch, Simeon went out to the pasture to check on Lena A. He found her standing off by herself. Simeon was sure it was close to calving time. He decided to take her to the special pen for sick cows at the front of the big barn. "It will be all right," Simeon said over and over as he led her into the barn. He put feed into the trough in front of the pen. He brushed Stella, the buggy horse. Then he checked on Lena again. Not much had changed.

Later, after supper, Simeon went out to help with the evening chores. When he got to Lena A's pen, he saw that she hadn't eaten the food that he had put in earlier in the day. Her eyes had that glazey look.

"Daat," Simeon yelled. "I think the calf is coming tonight. Lena A is off her feed. I want to sleep out here."

"That is fine, Son," *Daat* yelled back. He and Sylvan were washing up and sterilizing the metal milk buckets.

Simeon brought a flashlight, blanket, and pillow out to the barn and made himself a little bed on some hay. He settled in on the hay bales and stared at Lena A until his cheek bounced off his shoulder. He stood and shook himself all over, just as Ruff did after he got wet. He sat back down and propped his head in his hands, but he couldn't hold it. His head was aching. It wasn't long before he just didn't open his eyes anymore.

He heard the barn door creak open, and then he heard Stella's soft whinny. Stella was a chestnut-colored standardbred, a retired racehorse, only four years old.

Simeon opened his eyes. They felt gritty, like he'd rubbed some hay in them. He looked over at Lena A. She looked the same.

"Shh, there, girl," Simeon heard Sylvan say. It was Saturday night, so Sylvan had been out with his gang of friends. Simeon figured they had gone to a hoedown. That's what Sylvan had said they usually did.

At sixteen, Sylvan had begun *Rumspringa*—running around—the time when Amish youth can experiment with worldly practices. Simeon looked forward to *Rumspringa,* like every other boy he knew, but he didn't care that much about the socializing with girls, which also starts during that time. He knew that Sylvan did, though.

Maam said that Sylvan was just sowing his wild oats. She was sure he would settle down to the Amish way of life. Simeon wondered if she was right.

Now Simeon heard his brother lead Stella into the barn and then on into her stall. As Sylvan came out to hang Stella's halter on the barn wall, Simeon stood up and called quietly, "Sylvan."

"Simeon. What are you doing here?"

"Lena A," Simeon answered. Sylvan walked out of the barn, and Simeon followed him. He wanted to have Sylvan to himself, because that was rare these days, with his working and running around.

Sylvan went to the buggy and grabbed a pack of cigarettes. He headed out behind the small barn. He sat on the ground and leaned against the barn. Simeon did the same. Simeon watched as Sylvan lit the cigarette. He inhaled long and deep and blew out a long gush of smoke. He inhaled again, and blew the smoke out of his nose. After a minute, Sylvan said, "Lena A is calving now?"

"Ya," Simeon answered. "And I think something is not right."

Sylvan nodded.

"You are good at that smoking," Simeon said. He watched as Sylvan flicked ashes off with his little finger.

"Ya," Sylvan said. Sylvan was like *Grossdawdi.* He didn't say two words when one would do.

"Sylvan." Simeon waited while Sylvan finished the cigarette. "Have you thought of leaving?" Simeon meant leaving the Amish faith, which Sylvan could do at the end of *Rumspringa* if he decided not to be baptized and join the church. The decision would bc Sylvan's alone and made in his own time.

Sylvan stood up. He threw the cigarette on the ground and stamped on it with his shoe. "*Ya.* I'd like to have my own car." Sylvan knew it wasn't an issue to catch a ride in someone else's car, but owning one could cause problems. Speeding up life could disrupt community ways, and proud folks could show off their wealth.

"You've driven?" Simeon asked.

"*Ya.* Ben Stoltzfus's truck." Ben was their sixteen-year-old Mennonite neighbor. Sylvan whistled. "I drove so fast, the fields blurred. I left Lancaster County far behind.

"What about you?" Sylvan asked. "Have you thought about leaving?"

"I want more schooling." The words rushed out before Simeon had even thought them. He'd felt it for a while. To Simeon there was a whole world full of good things to learn, and he wanted to go beyond eighth grade, which is when the Amish stop going to school.

Sylvan clapped him on the side of the head, mussing his hair. "Only you would say that." Sylvan had whooped and hollered on his last day of school. He turned and walked into the small barn and put a ladder up against a wall. He climbed to the top and put the cigarette pack on a beam that joined there. He climbed down and moved the ladder back to its place.

Sylvan knew that Simeon was watching him. "You'll get your chance." His smile broke into a yawn.

Simeon stood, and looked down to hide his grin.

He stamped the ground with his bare foot to cover his happiness. This was Sylvan's cigarette hiding place, and Sylvan trusted him. Simeon didn't think his brother's smoking itself was much of a secret, because you could smell the smoke on him at times. When she passed him at breakfast after a night of running around, Lena was always wrinkling her nose, fanning her hand, and saying, "Whew."

This was the second secret of the day. Simeon smiled again as he thought about Little Elam and Mouse's milk. Little Elam had probably felt the same way he did right now.

Simeon said, "You better get inside. I reckon you got about four hours till milking." Sylvan turned and headed into the house. Simeon went back into the barn to check on Lena A.

Chapter 3

Simeon waited for another hour or so, but he had watched plenty of birthings before this one, and something wasn't right. He watched and listened to Lena A for a little more. She was pushing, but nothing was happening. He wished all his watching could help somehow, but it wasn't. He rubbed his head with his hands, and then he jumped up and ran for the house.

Simeon ran upstairs to his father's bedroom. "*Daat, Daat,* come," Simeon said as he shook his father's shoulder. "I think something is wrong."

"*Ya,* I will be right out," *Daat* said. When he got out to the barn, his mussed hair was standing up on the front of his head like a rooster's comb, but Simeon didn't feel like laughing. *Daat* checked Lena A and said, "I don't see the calf's legs." He reached into the cow. "And I don't feel the feet. I think we'd better call the vet. Could be it's twisted up inside there." He checked his pocket watch by the light of the lantern. "It's two in the morning, Simeon," he said. "You saddle up Stella and go over to the neighbors. You can call from there."

Simeon rode Stella up the farm lane and down the road to the nearest farm. They were Mennonites, and they had a phone in their house. Simeon quickly slid off Stella, not bothering to tie her, and ran to the door. He pounded on it until a sleepy-eyed Jim Stoltzfus answered it.

"Could you call the vet?" Simeon's voice caught in his throat, and he had to swallow hard.

"Slow down," Jim said. "What's wrong?"

"It's my cow, Lena A," Simeon said. "She's calving, but we can't see the calf."

"Okay, you head on home. I'll call the Doc. I'm sure he'll be right there."

Simeon rode home and went into the pen to stand by Lena A. "It won't be long now," he said.

He waited about thirty minutes for the sound of the car coming down the lane. He heard the bounce and then the metallic creak, thud as the car hit the potholes. I'd moan too, if I were that car, Simeon thought. The car shut off, and a door slammed.

Dr. Tom Brubaker strode into the barn. He was swatting flies with one hand and pulling something out of his pocket with the other. He had a stethoscope around his neck. Tom was a slight man. He wasn't tall, and he had short arms for a large animal vet. That's what he'd told Simeon, anyway. Sometimes he had to stand on a stool in order to get his arm down inside a big, old cow.

"Things not going well?" Tom asked as he pulled a long plastic sleeve over his arm. Simeon shook his head. "She's been pushing for hours now."

"Couldn't feel the legs," *Daat* said.

"Let's check things out here," Tom said as he examined the cow. "Looks like we need to cast the cow. The birth canal is twisted."

Simeon drew in a breath.

"It's okay, Simeon. We're going to put her down on her left side," Tom said. *Daat* came over, and Simeon watched as the Doc put a lariat around the cow's neck and legs and the two men laid her down.

"We need to get this calf twisted out. Bring me that plank over there, Simeon," Tom said. Simeon carried back the board, and Tom placed it over the belly of the cow. He stood on it, keeping the calf in place while *Daat* and Simeon turned the cow over, untwisting the birth canal.

"It's turning," Tom said. There was a whoosh as placenta water came out of the cow. Tom got down and checked the cow again. "We're going to have to pull the calf now."

Simeon heard the stamps and stirrings of the other cows. Simeon figured they knew something was happening.

They put Lena A in a frame with a clamp that caught her across the hips. Tom reached in and attached chains to the calf so they could pull it out. He ratcheted the handle to keep the chains tight. Sweat was running down Tom's face and arms. He began to manipulate the calf. Lena A was bawling.

Simeon stayed near Lena A's head, but he didn't take his eyes off Tom except to talk to Lena A now and then. “Trust Doc,” he whispered to her in between her bellows. “He knows what he is doing.”

Simeon blew out a long breath when the calf was finally out. “It’s a male,” Tom said. Simeon felt a twinge of sadness, because they wouldn’t keep the calf. They sold the male calves right away, only keeping the females, who would give milk.

The bloodied calf wasn’t breathing. “Here,” Tom said, and he handed Simeon a straw. “You tickle his nose and get him breathing.”

Simeon put a piece of straw up the calf’s nostril, and he half snorted a breath. They took the frame off Lena A, and it wasn’t long before she stood up and looked at her calf.

“Hey, Doc,” *Daat* called. “While you are here, could you look at these other two cows?”

“Sure,” Tom said, and he followed Elam Zook down the barn.

“You did good, Lena A,” Simeon said. “I knew you would.” He patted the cow’s neck and scratched her. “That was a long, hard birth,” he said as Lena A licked at her calf. “I’m sorry they will take your calf away soon, but the sooner the better. That way you won’t miss him so much.”

Simeon watched and laughed as the little calf tried to stand up. Then Simon sat down and laid his head on a bale of straw. He could hardly keep his eyes open. He'd only slept a few hours before Sylvan had come, and now it was almost time for milking.

"I know you will be a good milker, Lena A," Sylvan said. "You are so strong. You'll be giving milk for lots of years." Simeon was proud of her. He just sat in the pen and watched her and the little calf while Tom and his dad looked over the other cows.

"You've got a good one, there," Tom said. He looked at Lena A and then at Simeon.

"Ya," Simeon answered.

"You were watching me carefully. You always do," Tom said to Simeon. Tom started cleaning up while he stood by Lena A's pen. "I wanted to be a vet from the time I was a boy your age," he said.

"You did?" Simeon said.

"Yes. My father told me I had a way with animals. He said it was a gift from God, and I believed him."

"Did you learn from your father, then? Was he

a vet?" Simeon asked. Maybe he could go with Tom and learn from him.

"No, Simeon. He was a farmer. I learned farming from him, and I liked it. But I liked working with the animals best, so I went to college and then to veterinary school."

Simeon looked down and kicked the straw. He'd never be a vet unless he could get more schooling. What if he had a gift from God like Tom Brubaker? Would that make a difference in wanting to go on to school? God wouldn't give him a gift unless He wanted him to use it. Simeon would have to ask someone about it.

Tom headed toward the barn door. Simeon knew it was his job to fill the gallon buckets with water so that Tom could hose down his boots, so after saying goodbye to Lena A and her new calf, he headed outside. As Tom was washing his boots off, Simeon saw a light go on in his parents' bedroom window.

His mother came out the front door. She was a younger version of *Grossmudder,* but without the limp. *Maam*'s face was plain of feeling. Like most of the older Amish adults that Simeon knew, she rarely showed much emotion on her face, but she'd always had smiles enough for him. She folded her hands in front of her stomach.

"Where is your father, Simeon?"

"He's in the barn."

"Tell him his pager has gone off." Simeon's father was a firefighter with the small local fire company. All the rural fire companies in the area were volunteer, not governmental, so many Amish worked alongside the *Englisch.* They stopped their own work and joined in the firefighting, including riding trucks and manning the water lines. It was good for the community.

"Daat, Daat!" Simeon yelled as he ran toward the barn door. "There is a fire."

Chapter 4

Tom was still standing by his car when *Daat* and Simeon came out of the barn. "Do you want a ride to the station?" Tom asked. Elam Zook nodded and got in the car with Tom.

Lena came out of the house. It was time for the morning milking, and with *Daat* gone, she would have to help the boys in order to get all the chores done. She was dark-eyed and pert-nosed in the King family way, like her brothers, only her looks had been all brushed up and made into pretty. Her smile was wide and full of straight white teeth. All the boys had smiles full of jumbled-in teeth.

Simeon often wondered if Lena looked like his *Maam* had when she was young. He had no way of knowing because in the Amish way, there were no photographs.

"Hey, Arie, how's Lena A?" Lena asked Simeon. She always used her nickname for him.

"She is doing fine, but it was a rough one. She was twisted up, and Tom had to pull the calf, a heifer." Lena and Simeon walked to the pen where Lena A was standing. Simeon scratched Lena A. The little calf was beside her. The calf was pushing away, trying to stand up. Lena laughed as she watched the jerk, stumble of the calf's steps.

"You can do it, boy," Lena said. She watched for a few minutes and then turned to start the milking as Sylvan stumbled into the barn. "Better late than never, Sylvan. Was it a long night?" Lena said. "What was her name?"

Sylvan ignored Lena and turned to grab a milker, but Simeon laughed as he went off to feed the horses.

When Simeon was done with his chores, he got in the pen with Lena A. He scratched her head. She seemed to be doing fine.

"Do you think it was a big fire?" Simeon said to Jonas, who was still feeding the cows nearby.

"No," Jonas said. "It isn't *Dunnerwetter*—thunder weather—so it couldn't have been lightning. Besides, *Daat* says most of the fire calls are those nuisance calls, not the real thing."

"But maybe it was green hay. Maybe someone didn't let it dry and it started a fire."

"No, Simeon," Jonas said. He straightened his back, pushing both fists into it, and then picked up the wheelbarrow and headed back to the other side of the barn. "I doubt it. *Daat* will be back soon, you'll see," he called over his shoulder.

Lena came over and looked at the calf. "Looks like you're done, Arie. Let's go in for breakfast."

The air was lighter than it had been in a while, Simeon thought as they left the barn. Not so humid.

Simeon asked, "Do you think I have a way with animals, Lena?"

"*Ya,* sure," she said.

"Do you think it's a gift from God?" Simeon asked.

"I wouldn't say that, Arie. That is *Hochmut*—pride. *Demut*—humility—is our way."

Lena was going to be baptized in the fall.

Simeon knew that she was thinking about the ways of the church, the *Ottning,* a lot these days.

Simeon was starved. At the table he pushed his food in his mouth. Because it was Sunday, they wouldn't be doing farm work, and this was the off-Sunday, so there wouldn't be church. Simeon was relieved. In August, sitting for three hours in a house full of people was hard and hot. He pushed away from the table and went and lay on the rag rug in the parlor. It was a cool spot, cooler than anywhere else in the house. He stared at the corner cupboard, eyeing each piece of china and fancy glass dish. The grandfather clock in the corner ticked loudly but never chimed. It hadn't for years. His eyes moved over the hand-painted wooden chair to the roll-top desk, but no farther than that.

He fell into a cloudy sleep and watched a storm approach in his dreams. The thunder rumbled the cloud, and the cloud fought back with a flash and a switch of lightning. But the lightning hit their barn, which wasn't taking part in the fight at all. Why did the lightning do that? The question woke Simeon. He sat up.

He heard the grumble in his stomach. Now, that

is a rumble, he thought. So much for the storm. *Maam* must have let him sleep through dinner. She knew he'd had a long night.

Simeon heard the back door open. He wondered if his father had come home yet. "You look all played out, Elam," his mother said. "Here, sit. I'll get your dinner."

"It was a barn belonging to an Amos Dienner, down beyond Paradise. The barn is gone — *nunnergebrennt.* I stayed till the backhoes got done shifting the loads to make sure the fire was out," *Daat* said.

"And the animals?"

"We got them all out. They are in the heifer barn that Amos has across the road."

"Thank God for that," *Maam* said.

"I saw the old Amos. A *Grossdawdi.* He didn't move the whole last hour we were there. He just stared at the hole. Another man told me his grandfather built that barn."

"It's a pity," *Maam* said.

"It is so dry. They brought in at least a dozen fire companies."

It was quiet for a moment, and then Simeon

heard the sound of dishes and silverware rattling. His mom was putting the food on the table. Simeon got up to go into the kitchen, but the next words stopped him.

"What started it?" *Maam* said. "It wasn't lightning or wet hay. Was it carelessness, an accident?" She was quiet a moment. "Or could it have been one of the *Englisch*?"

"Hush, Rachel. It does no good to think that way."

"*Ya,* you are right, Elam. God will watch us, but an old, old barn. It's a shame." Simeon heard a clink in the sink.

"I must rest before milking. *Der Herr gibt und der Her nimmt* — the Lord giveth and the Lord taketh."

Simeon walked into the kitchen, and his mother dished up a plate of food for him.

Even though he'd slept so long during the day, Simeon had no problem falling asleep that night. Little Elam had to shake him awake the next morning.

Chapter 5

After breakfast, Simeon and Little Elam went to the big barn. *Daat* had said it was time for Little Elam to start feeding the ponies as well as the calves. But first, Simeon had something else to do.

He checked on Lena A. He rubbed her head, and she chewed away. He thought she was looking fine. "Doesn't she look good, Little Elam?"

"Ya, gut," Little Elam said.

Daat was finishing the hay cutting, while Jonas was raking the hay in the fields that had been cut on Saturday. By tomorrow, Simeon knew, they would be baling. He filled his chest with air as he felt his right arm muscle. Not too big, but big enough, he thought. He would be in on the baling this year.

"Now you wait down there, Little Elam. I will throw down the hay." Simeon climbed up into the haymow and threw down a bale of hay.

"Here you go, Starry and Blazer," he yelled. Simeon cleaned out the old hay and forked in the new. Little Elam watched, and then he gave each of the ponies their feed and water.

"Little Elam," Simeon heard his mother call from the garden when they'd finished feeding the calves. *Maam* and Lena were picking tomatoes. Simeon hurried back toward the big barn. He didn't want to get stuck in the garden this morning.

"Little Elam, you carry this bucket of tomatoes up to *Grossmudder,*" *Maam* said. Just before he stepped into the barn, Simeon glanced back and saw Little Elam tromp on a marigold at the edge of the garden as he lugged the heavy bucket of tomatoes.

Inside the barn, Simeon went into Stella's stall to brush her. He alternated between brushing and swatting flies. He heard the clip-clop of a horse and buggy in the lane. Simeon walked out of the barn to see his uncle Daniel hopping out of the buggy. His uncle Daniel was his father's oldest brother. There was only ten years between them, but Uncle Daniel looked like an old man. His lips were gray, and his eyes had shiny yellow folds below them. His white beard straggled, because he ran his fingers through it a lot. He pushed his gold wire-rimmed glasses up his nose every time he talked. Simeon wondered if too much sadness made people get old faster. Three of Uncle Daniel's seven children had died, one in a farm accident and two from illness.

"*Gut Marye,* Simeon. Is your *Daat* close by? We're heading to the horse auction. We're meeting Levi Blank there." Simeon had been with Uncle Daniel and *Daat* when they had picked Stella out at Levi Blank's farm. Daniel had looked at Stella and said that she wasn't sad, dull, or swaybacked. *Daat* had checked her teeth for her age and her legs for any sign of lameness. They had hooked her up to a wagon and taken her on the road to see if she was spooky. If she startled too easily when cars or trucks went by, that wouldn't be good. Buggy horses had to be on the road all the time. Stella had been a good buy.

"Are you looking for a horse to replace Mae?" Simeon asked.

"*Ya,* sure," Uncle Daniel said.

Simeon ran toward the fields and saw that his father was walking toward him.

"Is Daniel here?" he called.

"Ya," Simeon yelled back.

"Go find Sylvan and ask him to finish up for me. Jonas will finish the raking."

Simeon found Sylvan and gave him his father's instructions, and then he raced back to the buggy, where his father and Daniel were standing. Simeon asked, "Can I come with you?" He loved the horse auction. The last time he was there, an Amish boy was one of the riders who rode the horses in the auction barn when they came up for bidding. Simeon wished he could have a job like that.

"*Ya,* sure," his father said. "Someday you will know horses like your uncle Daniel does."

"That's about right," Uncle Daniel said.

During the hour it took to go the five miles to

the auction, Simeon couldn't help but ask, "Are we soon there yet?"

His father laughed and said, "Is Little Elam here with me?"

Simeon settled back and stared out the back window of the buggy at the car that was following them. They finally drove into the auction area, and Uncle Daniel pulled into the long shed built for the Amish buggies.

"Pretzel, *Daat*?" Simeon asked as they walked toward the horse barns.

"*Ya,* sure," his father said, handing him two dollars. Simeon stood in the long line outside the metal cart where they sold the big soft pretzels. It seemed like hours since breakfast. He chewed slowly as he walked into the horse barn. He stopped and looked into a room full of older Amish men playing checkers. He recognized a few of them and waved. Some waved, and some nodded.

Simeon walked into the main auction area and looked up and down the stands, but he didn't see his *Daat.* He wandered back to the stalls where people looked at the horses before they went onto the auction floor. Behind a wall, Simeon saw the draft horses. There was a line of eight or so. Uncle Daniel, his *Daat,* and Levi Blank, the Amish horse buyer, were talking to a small man dressed in blue jeans and a black leather vest and hat. The man was talking so quickly, Simeon was sure that his words were bumping into each other.

The man pointed to a gray Percheron. She was the same color as Butch, the horse they had at home. Simeon got close to his *Daat* and whispered, "Are you thinking of that one?"

"Ya," his father said. "Mares and geldings work good together. Look at Mae and Butch. What do you think?"

Simeon gulped down his last bite of pretzel and asked, "What's her name?"

"Dreamer," *Daat* answered.

Dreamer, thought Simeon. That's like me. I'm always wondering and dreaming about what's going to happen. Simeon walked over toward the horse. He slid in between it and the large brown horse standing beside it, and ran his hand up and down its side. He peered into the horse's mouth and looked at her teeth, as he'd seen Uncle Daniel do. He felt along the horse's legs, and picked up a hoof and looked at it. Simeon straightened up, and the horse tilted her head toward him and trembled. Simeon felt a tremor go down his arm, too. He rubbed the horse's great gray neck.

Levi put his thumbs inside the suspenders that stretched out to cover his large paunch and said, "Looking to take over my job someday, Simeon?" Everyone laughed as Simeon's cheeks burned.

Uncle Daniel said, "This one will do, Levi. I think she will take Mae's place."

Daat and Uncle Daniel went out to the auction area and climbed the wooden stands. After a while they started bringing in the draft horses. As they led them in, the ground shook. It wasn't long before the gray Percheron came in.

When the bidding began, there were three bidders. *Daat* kept nodding at the auctioneer's helper while the auctioneer yelled out the going price. The auctioneer's helper would yell out, "Hey," when a bidder nodded and then turn to look at the other bidders.

Simeon forgot to listen to the price because he was too busy watching the auctioneer's helper. Simeon soon realized that he was holding his breath after each one of *Daat's* nods and hitting his knee with his fist every time he heard the word "Hey," which meant the bidding kept going. He wanted *Daat* to get this horse.

When Simeon saw the auctioneer's helper look toward *Daat,* then look at the other bidders, and then look back at *Daat* without saying "Hey," Simeon knew the bidding was over. He drew in a long breath and filled his lungs clear up. When he heard the word "Sold," he blew his breath out loudly.

He watched as the auctioneer's helper took *Daat's* auction number. *Daat* and Uncle Daniel got up and headed back to the buggy. Simeon's sweaty shirt stuck to his back as he followed them along.

"That's a good thing, Daniel," Elam said. He stared up into the sky, shading his eyes. "And not a day too soon. We'll be baling hay tomorrow."

"Levi will see that the horse is delivered today."

Simeon had just finished his evening chores and was talking to Lena A when he heard the horse trailer drive into the lane. He grabbed a harness and rope and ran out to meet it. "Let me, *Daat,*" he said as his father walked toward the trailer.

His father took a long look at him and then said, "Go ahead, Simeon."

Simeon stepped up into the trailer and began stroking the big horse. He felt the tremors go from the horse down into his arms. Soon he began to whisper in its ear. "*Ach,* Dreamer. *Ach,* Dreamer, you're fine." Carefully, he slipped the harness on. The big horse was watching him, but Simeon felt the horse's trust in his hands before he looked at Dreamer's eyes.

Simeon led the horse out of the trailer and walked her into the barn and into the stall with Butch. Butch stamped a few times, but Dreamer just stood there as Simeon stroked her. "You'll do fine tomorrow when we begin the baling. I just know you will. You are my special horse."

All the horses turned and looked at the sound of Simeon's voice. Simeon had heard of a man who had lost his voice and had learned to handle all his draft horses just by the slightest touch. Simeon vowed that he would be able do the same thing one day. In fact, he told himself, he would be better than the man with no voice.

That night Simeon walked back toward the barn after checking on Dreamer one last time. He heard the low rolling twitter of the purple martins. He watched them flying in and out of the martin house. It had forty compartments.

He whistled as the evening settled around him with a deep purple iridescence, just like the color on a martin's head.

Chapter 6

The next morning after breakfast, Simeon stood with his father at the edge of the blue-gray alfalfa field. The heat was flickering up in tiny waves, but it wasn't humid and the dew wasn't too heavy. Sylvan was near the big barn, hitching up the horses. They used all six of the draft horses for baling hay.

"This is good weather for hay making," *Daat* said. He bent down and picked some alfalfa and rubbed it in his callused hand. He allowed it to drop between his thick fingers. "Feels dry."

"Do you think Dreamer will do all right?" Simeon asked.

"She'll do fine," *Daat* answered. "And what about you? Are you ready to throw bales?"

"Ya." Simeon stood straight. He was ready to take his place with the men. He heard the clip-clop of the horses and the creak of the hay wagon. The red and yellow New Holland baler was in place behind the diesel motor, which was mounted on the dolly behind the six horses. The two Percherons were on the right, and the Belgians were on the left.

Sylvan was standing up straight. He never sat when he drove the horses. His sleeves were rolled up, and Simeon couldn't help but see the muscles bulging in his forearms. When had Sylvan gotten so strong? Simeon looked down at his own rangy-looking arms and hoped they'd be strong enough to throw bales. His muscles looked more like pieces of thin rope. They didn't look as strong as they had just yesterday. He rubbed his shoulders.

Simeon and his dad climbed up on the wagon. With a click and a giddyap, they started off on their way around the field. The baler spat the bales down the chute one by one. It was Simeon's job to yank the bale that came down the chute and get it to his *Daat,* who would then stack the bales into a pyramid.

It wasn't long before Simeon was rubbing his eyes because of the bits of hay that stuck in them as the baler shot them out. The fumes from the motor were causing tickles in the back of his throat. Already his arms were tired. Behind him, *Daat* worked like a human machine. Simeon wished he was driving the horses instead of baling, but it would be a while before he got to do that. He'd only driven a two-horse team. Jonas had only started driving the big six-horse team in the spring.

They headed back to the barn with their first load of the day. Simeon took a long drink of the cool water from the thermos hanging off the back of the wagon.

They were almost done with their second load when Simeon heard Lena's voice. Simeon was relieved to hear her. It was lunchtime.

Sylvan pulled the horses to a stop. They were panting in the heat. Their sides were heaving. Simeon and *Daat* jumped off the wagon. Daat sat in its shadow, but Simeon walked up to the horses, who were still panting.

"You are great, Dreamer," Simeon said to the horse. Dreamer stamped her foot and swished her tail at a horsefly that looked as big as a dragonfly to Simeon.

Lena had a picnic basket, and Little Elam was carrying two jugs of mint tea. On his way out, he kept stopping and putting them on the ground. Ruff was walking beside him. Lena passed around the barbeque pork sandwiches and opened a bag of pretzels. There were apples and brownies for dessert. The apple helped quench Simeon's thirst just a bit. Lena unhitched the horses, and she and Sylvan led them to the water trough. It was a while before they came back. *Daat* drifted off to sleep, but Simeon couldn't. He kept swatting at a fly as he inhaled the sweet, pungent smell of the alfalfa. So much better than diesel fumes.

In the afternoon, during their third load, Simeon saw a rabbit jump away. He hoped that it didn't have a nest. His dad had told him about a snake getting caught up in a mower and what a mess that had been.

By the fourth load of the day, Simeon's elbow joints ached. He wasn't sure that his shoulders even remembered why they were attached to his body. Simeon wondered if Sylvan's neck hurt from looking over his right shoulder to make sure the baler was picking up the hay right. Clumps of hay at the corners of the field could choke up the baler.

Simeon kept telling his shoulders to lift, hold, swing. Lift, hold, swing. He pushed back his straw hat to the top of his forehead as the sweat rolled down. Grasshoppers leaped every which-a-way, and Simeon was glad for something to look at.

He couldn't believe it when he saw Sylvan turn and head toward the barn in the late afternoon. It was their fifth load. He'd made it through the day. Now he bent backward as far as he could, trying to stretch every part of his back. The horses were drenched with sweat. It looked like they'd been in a rain. Butch was frothy at the mouth.

Daat walked up and slapped Simeon on the shoulder. Simeon winced, but he smiled as *Daat* said, "A good day's work. We'll put it in the barn tonight."

After supper, Simeon did his evening chores. As he was finishing up, he heard a *thud, thud* on the side of the barn. When he went out, he saw Jonas throwing a softball against the side of the barn and catching it with his mitt. Jonas loved softball and played every chance he got. He had been hoeing tobacco most of the day.

Simeon didn't think his own shoulder could manage throwing a softball. He was tired. He couldn't believe that *Daat* and Sylvan were still putting up hay in the barn. Someday he'd be as strong as Sylvan.

Simeon went to the front porch and sat in a rocker next to *Grossmudder.* She was crocheting and rocking. Simeon listened to the roaring of the cicadas. They must fill the trees, he thought. As the evening darkened, Simeon watched the *Blitzkafer*—fireflies. Little Elam came out with a jar and ran around trying to catch them.

"Come, Simeon!" Little Elam shouted, "Help me."

"I'm too tired tonight," Simeon answered.

Simeon went inside a little earlier than usual and headed up to bed. It was hot upstairs, so he decided to sleep on the floor. He pulled his pillow off of the bed and lay down there. He was soon asleep.

Chapter 7

Simeon sat up.

It was still dark. His shoulders ached, and he felt a buzzing inside him. Simeon shook his head to make sure it wasn't the cicadas. Was everything all right? It didn't feel like it. He went downstairs and got a piece of bread and ate it. Then he listened. There was a stirring in the barn. He was sure of it. He should check on Dreamer. Perhaps the horse wasn't doing well after all.

Simeon grabbed a flashlight and checked the kitchen clock. It was a little past twelve. He walked outside and went toward the big barn. A bat swooped right above his head. Inside the barn, he went right to Dreamer's stall. The other horses stirred as Simeon passed. Dreamer looked up. Simeon stroked her nose and neck, while she stood absolutely still. Simeon couldn't see anything wrong with the horses.

The milking cows seemed fine, too. Simeon heard nothing beside the ordinary stamps and twitches. Maybe all the work today got to my head, Simeon thought.

As he headed outside, Simeon looked over at the small dry cow barn. Maybe something wasn't right in there. Simeon walked around, flashing his light here and there. Everything seemed fine. As Simeon turned to go, his flashlight beam hit the ladder, the one that Sylvan used to put his cigarettes up on the beam.

I wonder if they are still there, Simeon thought. I think I'll just check. It wouldn't hurt to look. Simeon climbed up the ladder and felt above the beam. He heard a plop as he accidentally knocked the cigarettes out of their hiding place. He climbed back down the ladder and picked up the pack.

He put his foot on the first rung of the ladder, and then he took it off. It really wouldn't hurt anyone, he thought. Just one cigarette. Besides, when he was sixteen, he'd be smoking just like Sylvan. He'd take his first one a little early. Simeon headed outside the small barn and sat down with his back against the wall. He sat in the very same place that Sylvan had. He lit the cigarette and took his first breath of it. He coughed. And then he heard something.

Chapter 8

It was a rustling. Or was it a crackling? It reminded Simeon of the bonfire they'd had last fall. But it was the middle of the night, and it was coming from the direction of the big barn. Simeon stood up and ran toward it. Then he heard a man's voice. It wasn't *Daat.*

"*Vas geh?* Who is there?" Simeon asked as he rounded the corner of the barn. Two strong flashlight beams blinded him. He couldn't see anything. He put a hand up to cover his eyes. The cigarette he'd been holding in his other hand dropped to the ground.

"Out for a smoke?" a voice said. "Well, you better forget that you ever knew anyone was here, because if you don't, we'll be back, and we'll burn your house down."

"Don't breathe a word to anyone. Ever. You got that?" another voice said.

Simeon's legs were trembling. He closed his eyes and leaned against the barn, sliding down the wall. He heard the crackle again, and this time Simeon was sure it sounded like a bonfire. He opened his eyes and saw two figures running away. Their clothes were dark. Simeon heard a crash, and the crackling became a roar. He looked up and saw flames coming out of the peak of the barn roof.

Simeon stared. Fear had his mind, stiffening his body until he couldn't move. Heat pressed through the barn wall, burning his arm. His bare feet were getting hotter. But still he couldn't move.

"Simeon, where are you?" It was Little Elam. Simeon saw that his little brother was running toward the barn. Then a loud pop from the fire stopped him, and he looked up, screaming, "Come out from the fire, Simeon!" And Little Elam went on screaming.

"*Gott* help me. *Gott* help me," Simeon whispered, and as his jaw moved, the numbness began to descend to his shoulders and then to the other parts of his body until it was gone. His legs stiffened, and he pushed up and ran toward Little Elam, grabbing his hand. "Come, come, Little Elam."

As they ran toward the house, he saw a light in his parents' bedroom and then he heard his father yelling. Better to take Little Elam to *Grossmudder's*, Simeon thought as the front door flung open. Sylvan ran out of the house, followed by Jonas and his father. "*Mache schnell!* Hurry!" *Daat* was yelling.

Simeon ran Little Elam around to the *Grossdawdi* house. He pounded on the door. *Grossmudder* opened it, and Simeon said, "Take him." He pushed his brother toward *Grossmudder.* Little Elam had not stopped screaming.

As Simeon turned and ran back toward the barn, he heard creaking and bashing. His chest squeezed. It was the horses kicking and pitching against their wooden stalls. He heard the bawling of the cows and an awful screaming, almost human. He knew it was the few calves in the big barn. "This isn't happening," he said. He couldn't help but repeat the sentence again and again.

"Get the animals out," *Daat* yelled as he and

Sylvan ran into the barn. Jonas, Lena, *Maam,* and Simeon followed them.

Simeon went toward Lena A, but *Maam* yelled, "We'll get the cows, Simeon. You get the horses." Simeon went to the horses as the others shooed the cows down, straining with the balky ones.

Simeon turned to the horses. "Go!" he screamed as he opened the stall doors. The horses reared and kicked. What could he do? What could he do? He ran out and got some rope that was hanging in the barn. He would have to slip ropes around them and lead them out.

Simeon gulped at the air as he led Dreamer to the hitching rail near the house. When he turned back toward the barn, he saw the flames jumping around the top of it. All the hay was curling into smoke. Three cuttings from the summer, and in fifteen minutes all the work was gone. His work of today was gone, too.

Jonas was bringing out two more horses. I must get the others, Simeon thought. He plunged back into the burning barn, feeling a searing heat on his face, his feet, and his hands. He brought Bob and then Cap out. He bent over, coughing and wheezing. The ponies, he thought. He hadn't seen Starry and Blazer.

Simeon uncurled and looked around. One more time, he thought. I must do it one more time. He ran back into the barn and found the little ponies. He led them out and over to the same area as the big Percherons and Belgians. And then Simeon fell on the ground and wheezed and wheezed.

A siren screeched. A fire truck pulled in, and the firefighters jumped out in their yellow uniforms. Simeon gasped when he saw the first plumes of water come gushing out of the hoses. They struck the barn with such force. Truck after truck pulled into the yard. It must be at least ten companies, Simeon thought. Water gushed in all directions. They were even spraying the house to make sure that if the fire leaped, it wouldn't catch it, too.

Simeon looked around, and when he didn't see Jonas, he tried to run into the barn again, but a fireman pulled on him and wouldn't let him. Simeon slumped to the ground by the barn. The ground was a huge patch of black muck and mud. His raw eyes ached. After a while he went to the pump and splashed water in them. He opened them, and then he closed them again to keep the smoke out. He felt water squeezing out of the corner of his eyes. He realized the water was tears, and he couldn't stop them. He opened his mouth and screamed. No one heard him as his voice blended in with the sirens.

He felt a touch on his shoulder. *Grossmudder* said, "Come, Simeon. You can't help here anymore, but Little Elam and I need you."

She led Simeon to the house. In her little kitchen by the stove, there was a big metal tub filled with water. Simeon took off his clothes and climbed into the tub. He scrubbed and scrubbed his skin. The water turned black. He wished he could scrub his mind. Get rid of the blackness there. Those voices, those words, the cigarette. Had he stomped it out? He couldn't remember.

Little Elam sat on the floor by the tub. He watched Simeon, and every few minutes, his body shook. "I'm sorry, Little Elam," Simeon said. It was his fault that his little brother couldn't stop trembling.

"I'm sorry," Simeon said again, remembering how Little Elam had come looking for him in the night.

"Hush, Simeon. We are all sorry. We are all sad right now," *Grossmudder* said. Simeon dried off and got into the clothes that *Grossmudder* had there. She must have gone to the house and gotten them for him. "Get in bed, Simeon. You too, Little Elam," she said.

Simeon climbed into *Grossmudder's* bed and wrapped his arms around Little Elam. Finally a darkness came. A darkness that had no orange, no flickering light. It was deeper than Little Elam's trembling body.

Simeon woke up and couldn't remember where he was. Then he heard the gurgle, cough of *Grossmudder's* snores. She was sleeping in the recliner so that he and Little Elam could sleep together in the bed. Simeon had slept in that recliner, himself, many times.

After *Grossdawdi* had died, *Grossmudder* had said that it had eased her heart to have Simeon there. He hadn't known what that meant then, but now he knew that a loving person could help just by being there.

He would never let anyone burn their house down. He couldn't.

Chapter 9

A scream came. And then another. Simeon was deep in smoky dreams. As he choked out of sleep, he realized it was Little Elam screaming, and screaming again.

Grossmudder was soon there standing by the bed. She picked up the little boy. "It's all right, Little Elam. Wake up. It's a nightmare." She carried him to her rocker. Simeon slipped out of bed and knelt beside them. The edges of light were just appearing though the window.

"I'm right here, Little Elam. The fire is gone. I'm right here," Simeon said. *Grossmudder* rocked him for a long time. When Little Elam was quiet again, she put him back in her bed. Simeon climbed in beside him and fell asleep.

Simeon sat up. It was quiet. No screaming. No shouting. No roar. No bawling, or grunting, or moos. No moos? What had happened to the animals?

Simeon got out of bed, leaving Little Elam, who was still sleeping. He didn't see *Grossmudder.* He opened the door and saw that it was late afternoon.

He walked around the house toward the barn and stopped. A square black hole filled the space that used to be the barn. Piles of blackened beams, stones, and metal were pushed around the silo, which was still standing. Simeon was amazed to see that the silo was still there. A bulldozer sat next to the piles, and the red and yellow baler, all blackened by soot, was sitting in the field behind the hole.

His *Daat* was standing by the hole. Two old men were standing on the other side of the hole next to the bishop, Ben Fischer. Simon squished through the mud in his bare feet toward his father. "*Geb acht*—watch out," his father said.

The scorched smell filled Simeon, burning his nose and throat, and he coughed. He felt an ache in his shoulders and back, and he wondered what it was from. With a jolt, he realized it was from baling hay. He couldn't believe that just this time yesterday, he had been throwing his first bales of hay.

He stood next to his father. They stared quietly for a few minutes. *Daat* had a look of Uncle Daniel this morning. His lips were gray. Would *Daat* carry the sorrow like Uncle Daniel? I can't let that happen, Simeon thought. "The animals?" Simeon asked.

"We got them all out, Simeon. The ponies and Stella are in the small barn with the dry cows."

"And where are the milking cows and the other horses?"

"They are down the road at Jacob Lapp's." Jacob had sold his cows the year before. He still had a few, but most of his time was spent helping his wife run their quilt business. They sold quilts to the tourists who came to the county to see the Amish.

"It's good for us that he sold his cows," Simeon said.

"Ya," his father answered.

"Who are the men over there?" Simeon asked.

"They are the men from the Aid who will help with the barn raising," *Daat* answered. Simeon nodded. "Ben thinks they can have it rebuilt in three weeks."

"But the hay, *Daat.* It's all gone." Simeon felt a touch on his arm. Little Elam was standing beside him. Simeon took his hand.

"Yes, it is, Simeon. We will have to buy hay and feed, but that is my part to think about, Simeon, not yours." *Daat* patted Simeon on the shoulder. "Go feed the ponies and the dry cows. The other boys and Lena are still down at Jacob's. I must talk." *Daat* strode away toward the men on the other side of the hole.

Simeon and Little Elam went into the small barn to feed the dry cows. Little Elam fed the ponies. When they came out of the barn, Little Elam fed the calves. He was quiet the whole time. Simeon saw two buggies turning down the lane. A black car pulled in behind them. Two women got out and headed up to the house with pans in their hands. Some men headed over toward *Daat.* These people had come to help with the cleanup.

Then another vehicle pulled in. It had the words STATE POLICE on the outside. Why would the police come? Simeon wondered. The firemen had put out the fire.

Simeon went into the house and sat at the table in the kitchen. *Grossmudder* was moving about as usual, but *Maam's* shoulders were sagging a bit.

Grossmudder set a plate of eggs and toast in front of Simeon. She poured him a glass of milk. She buttered his toast and puts lots of strawberry jam on top. Simeon stared at his plate.

"Eat, Simeon," *Maam* said. Simeon did, but he felt he was chewing paper. He wondered if the smoke had scratched his tongue and his throat until all his taste buds were gone. Maybe he would never taste again.

Jonas sat beside him dipping his toast into the egg yolk. He put the whole piece of toast in his mouth and grabbed another. He poured himself a bowl of cereal, and he gulped hot black coffee as he ate it. Simeon watched him instead of eating.

Could they be sitting in the same house? Were they in the same family? How could Jonas eat? Simeon pushed back from the table, and his chair fell backward. *Maam* cried out and covered her mouth with her hand.

"Simeon, are you all right? You haven't touched your food." She hurried over as Simeon bent to pick up the chair. When he stood up, she placed her hands on his shoulder. "Sit down, please." Jonas kept eating.

Simeon turned and pushed the chair under the table. "My throat hurts. I'm not hungry." Am I so different, then, Simeon thought? Is it just me? But Jonas had not heard what he heard that night in the barn. Jonas had not seen what he saw. Simeon realized that he didn't want Jonas to see what he'd seen. Simeon shivered in the hot kitchen.

Simeon's father walked into the kitchen. At his side was a broad-shouldered man in a short-sleeved uniform. Thick hair covered his arms. His forehead was small, and his eyes were round, but his large square jaw had a beard shadow. He is a bull, Simeon thought, not a man.

"This man is the state police fire marshal," *Daat* said. "Lena, could you take Little Elam outside?" *Daat* looked at the fire marshal and said, "The little boy is afraid."

The man's eyes followed Lena as she and Little Elam walked out. "I will want to speak to her later," the man said. "I'm here to investigate this fire. This is the second barn fire in the last two weeks. We can't ignore the fact that they could have been set." The man drew his brows and broke off his sentence.

The man's words had pulled the air from the room. In its place was a smell. It was dark and musky. It stayed in the room, reminding Simeon of the smell of the dead shrew that Mouse had brought in not long ago. A fear smell.

"When we suspect arson, we need to get all the information we can. If anyone saw anything or knows anything, he or she must tell us." The fire marshal looked from person to person as he talked.

Simeon dropped his eyes long before the fire marshal could look at him. His right hand felt hot. Burning hot. He could feel the cigarette burning a hole right through it. He rubbed the palm with his index finger. A pain shot up his arm and through his body as he rubbed his hand.

"But why would someone do that?" Jonas asked. "Set a fire?"

"For all sorts of reasons. Some people set fires to

get insurance money, but I realize that isn't the case with you Amish. Sometimes it's firebugs."

"Firebugs?" Jonas asked.

"People who love to set fires." The man paused and cleared his throat. "But as these fires have been on Amish farms, we have to consider that it could be someone who doesn't like the Amish."

Simeon was looking at *Grossmudder,* and he saw the man's words knock the air from her. Simeon saw her face flatten and her mouth drop open. Sylvan was open-mouthed, too. They looked like fish, Simeon thought, hooked and left on the ground by the pond. Should I say something? Simeon thought.

Simeon turned and looked at his father and saw the yellowy shine on his face. *Daat* was looking even more like Uncle Daniel. Simeon saw the quiver in his mother's left hand and her stooped shoulders, and the bulging pulse in the right vein in Jonas's cheek. His fear drained down through his feet. His legs slackened, and he felt a weight in his ribs. His chest ached, fierce with a heavy love.

No, he thought quickly. He could never let

anything happen to them. There was no doubt in his mind that the fire setters would harm them. None at all. He knew they would come and burn their house. And he couldn't let them do that to his family. What if they burned one of them this time?

The man's words on the night of the fire swirled in Simeon's mind and he wanted to shout them out, but instead he pushed them deeper inside, down into his aching chest. Surely it was the best way for them all. He was keeping them safe, wasn't he?

Simeon's stomach started cramping. He wanted to run to the bathroom. Please leave, he silently pleaded to the fire marshal. I don't think I can sit here much longer. Please, please.

The fire marshal turned and walked toward the door. "I'll be back later, when you've had time to think. I'm sorry to be so blunt, but time is important for us."

Simeon ran to the bathroom. He curled into a little ball on the floor between the sink and the toilet and cried until the cramping in his stomach stopped.

Chapter 10

When Simeon went outside, lines of volunteers were forming beside the blackened barn hole. Charred wood, twisted metal, and stones were being hauled out of the hole, then handed up and over, passed along from one person to the next.

Simeon moved with the others. Hand to hand, he said over and over in his head. He was a helper. He was just one of them. Not someone who knew something. Little Elam stood behind him without saying a word. Just watching. Then he sat down and watched Simeon until he fell asleep.

Simeon worked until supper. Everyone ate outside. There were dots of people all over the lawn. He wiped the sweat from the fold in his neck.

Little Elam sat next to Simeon during the meal. Afterward, Little Elam wandered up to the front porch of the house and lay down in the porch swing. Lena came out of the house and sat next to him. After a while she got up and came down to where Simeon was sitting on the grass.

"He is affected, Simeon," Lena said. "In his head. Something is wrong, I think."

"Just *darichnanner* — confused," Simeon said. He had nothing more to say to Lena about Little Elam.

It was time for the evening chores. Simeon called Little Elam, who had not left the porch swing. Together they walked to the small barn. While Simeon fed the dry cows, Little Elam watched.

Little Elam walked outside of the barn to feed the calves. Simeon was finishing up his work when he looked over and saw the ladder. If only he hadn't climbed that ladder. If only he'd gone back inside. As Simeon was staring up at it, he realized that he didn't remember what he had done with the pack of cigarettes. Had he left them outside by the barn?

Simeon ran outside and went to the wall where he had sat the night before. The cigarettes were lying there. Simeon looked around, but he didn't see anyone. He picked the cigarettes up and stuffed them down in his pocket under his handkerchief.

He went back into the barn. He laid the pack of cigarettes in a corner and stomped on them. He carried several bales of hay over and stacked them on top of the crushed pack. That would have to do for now.

When he was done, he looked up and saw Little Elam standing in the doorway of the barn. How long had he been there?

"Let's go over to Jacob's and check on Lena A," Simeon said. Simeon was glad that someone had pulled out a saddle and halter for Stella before they got burned up. Simeon saddled up Stella and pulled Little Elam up behind him.

"We're going to Jacob's," Simeon yelled to Sylvan as they went down the lane. The horse's hooves clipped in a neat, even beat. Jacob's farm was a mile away.

Simeon left Stella at the hitching rail and walked toward Jacob's barn. Jacob Lapp waved to them from the field. Simeon waved back. Little Elam walked toward the sheep that were out in the pasture where Jacob was.

When Simeon got in the barn, he found Lena A. She was chewing, head down. "Firebugs, he called them. *Blitzkafer.* The fire marshal said they loved to set fires," Simeon said to Lena A.

The cow swished her tail and put her head down to the feed trough. "I'm not a firebug, but I was out there smoking that cigarette. I probably have to tell someone. I dropped it, and I can't remember if I stomped it out. Maybe it added to the fire. I don't know."

Simeon wiggled his foot on the barn floor, worrying the hay all around. "That fire marshal said there are people who don't like the Amish. Jonas told me about that once. He said some people do things just because of hate. Hate crimes, he called it. He said they set fires to Amish barns a long time ago, somewhere up north." Lena A stamped her right back hoof.

"What should I do? I know the firebugs will come back and hurt us if I say anything. They said they would burn the house down, and I believe them. I couldn't bear for anything else to happen to anyone." Lena A kept chewing. Simeon slapped her side.

"You are doing fine," he said. "Better than I am, Lena A." Simeon wondered if cows had nightmares of fire and smoke. If they did, he couldn't see any signs of it in Lena A.

Simeon heard a kick in a stall. "That might be Dreamer," Simeon said. He walked until he found her. Simeon whispered to the big horse as he went in the stall. The horse settled, and Simeon ran his hand along her side.

As Simeon and Little Elam headed home, Simeon asked, "Do you want to catch the *Blitzkafer* tonight? I'm sorry I was too tired before."

Little Elam just shook his head.

When they got home, they sat on the front porch swing and rocked with *Grossmudder.* Once again, the cicadas screamed as the sun slowly dropped from the sky. The lavender sky deepened to violet. How can so much stay the same, when so much changes? Simeon thought. He and Little Elam went up to bed and were soon asleep.

Chapter 11

Little Elam screamed. "Simeon, Simeon, come out from the fire," he called out. He screamed again. It was the first time he had spoken in hours, and he was still asleep. Jonas and Sylvan jumped out of their bed and were running across the room as Simeon shook Little Elam.

"Wake up, wake up," Simeon said. "It's a bad dream, Little Elam." Oh, I need to help you, Simeon thought. Little Elam trembled so hard his lips shook, and he blinked as tears streamed down his face. His shaking was worse than the night before.

Maam appeared in the doorway with a gaslight. She put the light on the dresser and sat on the bed.

She stroked Little Elam's hair back from his sweaty forehead. Simeon slipped out of bed and walked to the window.

"You slept with him last night, Simeon. Was he like this at *Grossmudder*'s?" Simeon did not turn around. He clutched the windowsill with both hands.

"Ya," he said.

Please get better in your head. Please. Simeon sent his thoughts across the room. He went downstairs and out the front door. The moon was bright, and the lawn was full of shadows. He stared at the moon for a while, and then he went back into the house and fell asleep on the sofa.

In the morning after chores, Sylvan and Simeon took the buggy to Jacob Lapp's. Together they piled bales of hay on Jacob's wagon. They needed more hay for the dry cows, calves, and ponies. They also needed more feed, even though some silage had been saved in the silo. Sylvan lifted the bales of hay up to the cart. He whistled as he worked. Simeon piled them in a pyramid as he'd seen his father do.

"Sylvan, have you ever had a secret you didn't tell anyone?" Simeon asked.

"Sure. Doesn't everyone?"

"Ya," Simeon answered. "I guess so, but I mean something that you are afraid to tell?"

"Because I think it will get me in trouble, you mean?" Sylvan said.

"Sorta," Simeon answered, thinking about the cigarette, but then he thought about the men's threat. "But what if it's more than that, too. I mean, what if the truth could get someone hurt?"

"Well...sometimes the truth does hurt." Sylvan laughed. "Especially if the truth gets you punished."

"No!" Simeon raised his voice; he was almost shouting. "That's not what I mean. You don't get it."

Sylvan dropped the hay bale he was holding. "What's wrong, Simeon?"

"Nothing," Simeon whispered. He paused a moment, then went on: "Sylvan, have you ever been really scared?" He couldn't remember Sylvan being scared.

"Remember the first year that I was driving while we were baling hay?"

"Ya," Simeon answered. It was easy to remember because Sylvan had broken his leg that summer.

"Well, I forgot to look exactly where the ditch was when I was turning the horses. As we began to turn, I felt the sliding, and I was terrified. *Daat* was on the wagon behind me."

"What did *Daat* do?"

"He yelled, but it was too late. He was thrown off and so was I. He was sore, but I ended up with a broken leg," Sylvan said.

"Did *Daat* ever say anything to you about it?"

"No."

"And he put you back up at the end of the hay season when you got your cast off."

"Ya," Sylvan answered.

"Were you afraid then?"

"*Ya,* but *Daat* said, 'Sylvan, the best thing is to get back up. You know what you need to do.'"

"And you didn't want to let him down."

"Ya," Sylvan said. He stared at Simeon until Simeon looked away.

"You're a good driver now," Simeon said. "Looks like we're almost done." He kept his eyes down, and he watched Sylvan's feet as they turned away. They finished loading the hay. Sylvan went to get the horses to hitch them to the wagon.

It was quiet in Jacob's barn. The cows were in the pasture, and Jacob's horses were out working. A barn swallow swooped over Simeon and landed on a mud-plastered nest. Simeon could see the hay sticking out of the layers of mud in the nest.

"Giddyap," Sylvan said to the horses, and the wagon lurched out of the barn. Simeon was quiet as they drove the wagon back to the farm. Sylvan would walk back to get the buggy later in the day.

Simeon and Sylvan went to the little barn and unloaded the hay. Then they both went and got back into the cleanup lines. Little Elam sat on the front lawn and watched them as they worked.

By the evening meal, Simeon's shoulder muscles ached. He hadn't done so much lifting in all of his life. It was worse than the first day of baling. After supper, he and Little Elam went out to the smaller barn to do evening chores. The older boys and *Daat* were down at Jacob Lapp's. The women were still inside, doing up the mounds of dishes that had been used to feed all the people.

When Simeon was done with the feeding, he looked over and saw Little Elam standing between the two ponies.

"Where is the pony cart?" Little Elam asked. It was the first thing he had said while he was awake in the last two days.

"I'm afraid it burned up. I don't think they could save it."

Little Elam started to cry. Simeon went to him and hugged him. "You wanted to learn to drive it, didn't you?"

Little Elam nodded.

"We had a good first lesson the other day. Remember?" Simeon said.

Little Elam nodded again.

"I'm sure we'll get a new one," Simeon said, even though he doubted it. Money would be going to other things like hay and feed. "Maybe the new pony cart will be yours."

After chores, Simeon rode Stella down to Jacob Lapp's. The cows that were in the pasture stopped grazing and stared at him. In another part of the pasture, the draft horses were standing together. Dreamer, the new draft horse, raised her head and looked toward Simeon.

Simeon remembered that he'd been going out to see her on the night of the fire. She'd been fine then, but he wondered how she was now. He walked out to the big horse and ran a hand over her back and her legs, checking her out. As he did, he started talking.

"I don't know what to do, Dreamer. I've shared secrets with Little Elam and Sylvan in the last week, but this is different. This secret feels too big for me. Should I share it? With someone besides you, I mean." Simeon laughed. "I'm trusting you won't breathe a word to anyone."

Simeon stroked the horse. "*Daat* told Sylvan, 'You know what you need to do.' And Sylvan did. But I don't know what to do. I don't know what's right anymore."

The horse was motionless. Simeon left his hand on her neck and stilled himself to listen for the quiet inside him. He couldn't seem to reach it anymore. He heard the stamp of other cows. One bawled out. They were restless.

He left the pasture, went back in the barn to see Lena A, and rode back home. The night was sticky, and the weather was shifting. We need a good storm to blow this all away, he thought.

After putting Stella in her stall, Simeon came

out and lay on the grass in front of the house. On the porch, Lena was reading a Little Bear book to Little Elam, who was leaning his head on her shoulder. Simeon saw Little Elam's head falling into Lena's lap. She pulled the book up and kept reading until she'd finished it. Simeon listened to the cicadas and the swoop of the martins, but there was no safety in the sounds. How could these sounds ever be safe again? Simeon couldn't trust them anymore. They could be hiding things. He sat up and hugged his knees.

Maam came outside. She picked up Little Elam to take him to bed, and Simeon followed her, watching her broad back. *Maam* walked lightly up the stairs. She was strong, inside and out, Simeon thought. He wished he could be carried in her arms again, but even she couldn't carry him away from his thoughts. She gently undressed Little Elam after she laid him on the bed. Little Elam murmured but didn't wake up. Simeon undressed and climbed on the bed, too. His brothers would come in later.

They were all asleep when Little Elam cried once again, "Simeon, Simeon, come out from the fire!" Jonas jumped out of bed and came over to

Little Elam. Jonas held Little Elam as Simeon struggled to wake up.

Simeon stared at the ceiling, fixing himself inside the crack that he looked at every night.

If he told them what had happened, would it help Little Elam? Sweat beaded on Simeon's upper lip. He wiped it with the back of his left hand. Simeon heard a sound in the doorway. *Maam* was standing there.

Simeon opened his mouth to say, *I was out there,* but then the voice shimmered in his mind with rising waves of heat: "We'll burn your house down. Don't breathe a word to anyone. Ever."

Maam crossed the room and put her hand on Little Elam's head. "He's running a fever," she said. She picked up Little Elam and took him out of the room. Simeon heard her footsteps as she carried him to her own room.

Simeon licked his lips. They were chapped. He closed his mouth, but his parched throat wouldn't let him swallow. He grabbed his flashlight and went downstairs to the kitchen to get something to drink. He heard steps behind him.

Sylvan walked up beside him and got a glass of

milk. When Simeon glanced at him, he was scratching his chin, right in the cleft. Simeon had seen him do this lots of times before. He was thinking deep. "If there is something you want to tell someone, Simeon, you can talk to me. I been thinking about your questions in the barn."

Sylvan's words made Simeon wonder if he'd said too much to him.

"*Ya,* sure," Simeon said.

Sylvan turned and walked out of the kitchen. Simeon heard the creak of the stairs, even though he was sure that Sylvan was stepping in the middle of each board in the worn spaces. Simeon heard his mother's muffled voice. He heard the shuffles, and the grate of wood as his brother got into bed.

Simeon got his glass of milk and sat down at the table. It was three in the morning. In two hours they'd be milking. He downed his milk and then laid his head on the cool table surface. How could love hurt so much?

Simeon thought he heard a beeping. Then the sound came again. It was coming from his father's room. It was his pager. There was a fire.

Chapter 12

Simeon jumped up and ran out the back door. Without the barn, he had a clear view way down the road. There was a glow. A glow that shouldn't be there. It was in the direction of Jacob Lapp's farm.

No. No. No. Not again. Simeon's thoughts squeezed his mind like his last straw hat that had gotten too small. He couldn't move. He heard a pounding in the house. The front door flung open, but Simeon didn't run to the front of the house. He was staring at the glow.

He heard Sylvan's voice. "Look there. In the direction of Jacob's. Is the fire there?"

"Hitch the buggy!" *Daat* yelled.

Sylvan ran toward the small barn, and Simeon felt his legs finally beginning to move, to run, too. They had more sense than his mind. Simeon held Stella while Sylvan hitched her up. Sylvan stared down at Simeon's bare feet.

"Get your boots," Sylvan said. Simeon ran to the back door of the house and yanked it open. Jonas was pulling up a suspender as he ran by Simeon. When Simeon got back to the buggy, *Daat* was climbing in with his fire gear.

"Go straight toward the fire," he said to Sylvan. Sylvan slapped the reins, and they took off.

By this time, the orange glow in front of them had the look of swirls. It was flames. It was Jacob's place. The roaring sound was getting louder than the clip-clopping of the horse. A siren blared behind them. Simeon covered his ears. A fire truck was honking behind them when they turned into Jacob's.

Jacob was running toward the barn. His hair was skewed and standing up in all directions. "The animals!" he yelled. "The horses and a few cows were in the barn. Most were out in the pasture last night."

Daat yelled, "Get the horses!" but Simeon wasn't listening. He just ran into the barn yelling, "*Wo bist du?* Where are you?" Lena A had been in the barn last night when Simeon had come to see her.

Simeon ran wildly, knocking into a rail. He spun off it and fell over a hay bale. "Lena A?" He coughed as the smoke filled his open mouth. His eyes were so runny, he couldn't see. Simeon could hear a shrill screaming sound. He knew it must be some cows.

He stood, and there was an explosion, followed by a whoosh of air to the right side of him. It knocked him backward. There was a line of fire where the horse stalls had been. Simeon covered the right side of his face, which felt scorched. He felt a jerk on his arms. He was being lifted over someone's shoulder. His arms hit the oxygen tank on the fireman's back. The fireman strode out of the barn and laid him on the ground.

"Stay out here," he said.

Simeon coughed and coughed. His ribs ached. He couldn't sit up, so he watched the firemen from his dad's company while lying on the ground. They must have come when he was in the barn. They would be among the first to get there since they were the closest. Simeon could see his father standing by the truck operating the controls for the hand lines.

For a long time, Simeon lay there without moving. He kept hearing the explosion, feeling the whoosh of air sucking the fire into the barn, seeing the wall of fire.

You are still alive. The words were in his brain, but it was like someone else was speaking them. It was like a voice on Sylvan's radio reporting the news, but the radio was in Simeon's head.

Simeon heard more fire trucks pull in. Men sprayed hoses and yelled, but it all just swirled around Simeon like the smoke swirling around and up from the barn.

"Hello there, Simeon. It looks like they've gotten things under control." Simeon squinted up at Tom Brubaker, wondering if that were true. Simeon had no idea about the fire. The sky was etched with the spider webs of sunlight through cloud. It was sunrise.

"You aren't looking too good. Did you go in the barn?" Tom asked. Simeon nodded. Tom sat on the wet grass beside Simeon. He placed a large bag on the ground beside him. "I had to walk in here, because I couldn't drive with all the fire hoses lying around. Must be eight to ten fire companies here."

Simeon didn't reply.

Tom went on, "Someone called me, and Jacob got on the line and said that he was afraid there were some animals in the barn. Is this where your animals are being kept now?"

Once again, Simeon nodded.

"Oh, Simeon, I'm so sorry." Tom glanced over at the hitching rail. It was full of horses. Some were tied to a fence nearby. "It looks like they got the horses out."

Simeon pushed with both hands until he was sitting up. He'd forgotten everything, even why he had run into the barn. He saw the horses and sagged back to his elbows with relief. Maybe it would be all right. Maybe Lena A was in a pasture, or had been in a pen. He lay back down, pressing his scorched cheek into the wet grass.

"Is that your dad over there by the truck?" Tom asked.

"Yes," Simeon croaked. It was all the voice he had.

Two firemen came rushing toward the fire truck. They were yelling at the men with hoses. Both Simeon and Tom heard the word *cow.* Tom jumped up, yelling, "I'm the vet." He walked over toward the fire truck. Simeon followed him.

"We found a cow still alive," a tall, thick fireman said to Tom. "She was at the back wall of the barn where it banks into the hill, along the rear stone wall. A lot of the structure had fallen around her, but we were able to get her out. She's lying down out back." The fireman turned toward Simeon's father. "Here, let me help you with the hoses. We've done all we can at the back."

Simeon had heard that voice before. It was a young man's voice. Simeon stopped.

Another voice spoke: "Apparently the cow was able to get enough fresh air from the draft that was caused by the fire pulling air along the back wall of the barn. Of the rest down there, five or six were dead. Looks like they suffocated."

Simeon knew that voice, too. Think, he said to himself. Where had he heard these men?

"Somehow this one didn't get struck by anything. This one must be a survivor. You got to do something, Doc." The second voice was heading around to the back side of the barn. Simeon turned and saw blond hair sticking out of the bottom of the fireman's helmet.

Simeon looked down as the blond fireman walked back by him toward the fire trucks. He could see the cow lying on a patch of grass behind the barn. Much of the hair was singed off its back, and instead there were splotches of ash. Simeon smelled the burned flesh, and he saw the burnt skin on the cow's neck. He covered his nose and breathed through his mouth.

When he and Tom reached the animal, Simeon dropped to his knees. A harsh cry, like the caw of a crow, came out of his raw throat. It was Lena A. He hadn't even recognized her because of how horrible she looked. Her breathing was labored. She was panting, with her tongue hanging out. Each breath was a struggle.

"She's going to make it, Doc, right? They said she is a survivor," Simeon's voice rasped out. He put his hand on Lena A's side.

Tom put his stethoscope on. "Her lungs sound really bad, Simeon. Her heart rate is extremely rapid. She took in too much smoke. She won't make it, Simeon. I need to do what is best for her. Is that all right with you, Simeon?"

Simeon's throat was thick; he couldn't speak. He just nodded. Tom put the halter on her head and tied her head to her rear leg. He gave her the shot, and Lena A lost consciousness, relaxed, and stopped breathing. Tom took the halter off and listened to her heart. He stood up. It was over.

Simeon took his hand off Lena A. He stood and turned away from Tom. He scratched at the tears running down his scorched face. He kicked a chunk of burning wood that wasn't far from Lena A. He hated fire. He glanced up and saw the blond fireman. Suddenly a memory formed.

Dark, flashlight, laughter, smoke . . . but it couldn't be. He felt a sour taste come mashing up his throat. He turned and ran back to the grass, dropped to his knees, and threw up. He wiped his mouth and settled back on his knees.

He shook his head back and forth like the workhorses did when they were getting the bits settled right in their mouths after drinking water. He was getting his thoughts just right. It couldn't be, but it was. These firemen had set the barn fire at his house. Maybe they had set this one, too. Had they seen him standing there behind Tom? No, he didn't think so.

He hated those firemen. It was their fault. Their fault. A searing pain exploded inside of him. It was like the burning wall of fire in the barn. It raced through him, filling him with a white heat.

He streaked around the barn and straight over to his dad's company fire truck. The tall, thick fireman and the blond one were spraying with hoses. Simeon grabbed the hose from the blond fireman and turned it on the other man. The force of the water threw Simeon backward as it blasted the tall fireman, who yelled and dropped his own hose. The blond fireman shouted and grabbed the hose out of Simeon's hand. Simeon jumped up and began beating on the back of the blond man with both of his fists.

"Simeon, stop, stop!" *Daat*'s voice pierced the white heat that held Simeon. Simeon felt hands pulling on him. Tom was pulling Simeon into himself. He held Simeon from behind in a giant bear hug, while Simeon punched the air. Finally, Simeon's fists fell to his sides.

"It was Lena A," Tom said to Simeon's father, who hadn't moved from the fire truck. "I had to put her down." Simeon felt his father's eyes, but he wouldn't look up at him.

Tom released him, and Simeon took two steps toward the horses, but his rubbery knees didn't work too well. He slipped in the mud and fell forward, then caught himself and laid his head on Butch. He wrapped one arm under the horse's neck, and with the other he stroked the horse. Simeon felt the quiet. His breath slowed.

Chapter 13

Sylvan was at the hitching rail with Stella. "Let's go home, Simeon," he said. When Sylvan had the buggy hitched up, Simeon slowly walked over and climbed in. They were silent during the ride. Simeon felt his head bang against the side of the buggy several times.

When they got home, Simeon went inside and washed, but no matter how he scrubbed, he smelled of burnt cow flesh. It was in his hair, his arms, his hands. Maybe it was in his soul, oozing out through his skin. He dressed and walked out of the house. He headed along the fencerow.

He walked at the edge of two plowed hay fields. They could get in one more plowing, but they'd have to borrow the equipment. Most everything had burned up. Little dog-teeth burrs stuck to his pants. He passed a groundhog. It was not ten feet away, but it didn't move. Farther down the field, Simeon realized that the crows hadn't dive-bombed him.

Killdeer. Simeon stopped as he heard the bird say its name. Not a foot away from him he saw a killdeer hobbling away, dragging its wings as if they were broken. Simeon knew they weren't broken. The bird was drawing Simeon away from its nest. Simeon spotted the shallow hollow of a nest on the ground and stepped around it.

"You did a better job than I did," Simeon said to the killdeer. Simeon felt his anger draining away as he watched the bird. He had tried to drag his wings, to keep the bad away, but it hadn't kept Lena A safe, and Simeon now knew he couldn't keep his family safe either, no matter how much he loved them. Sadness swelled inside him. When he looked up from watching the killdeer, the field and sky were tinged with gray. It was like looking through a screen door, except the wire was so fine you couldn't even see it. Simeon thrust his hands deep in his pockets.

He got to the little creek that divided *Daat*'s

farm from Eli's. He sat on a rock and watched the water. A dragonfly buzzed all around him. He saw a whirligig beetle and a backswimmer. He settled on some rocks at the edge of the creek and tried to scoop up the water striders that went skidding by. He caught one and released it.

Last year at this time, *Daat* and Simeon and his brothers had gone fishing two mornings in a row after milking. The third hay harvest had been in, and school had been about to start the next week. If only it was last year, Simeon thought. Lena A would still be here.

"Where will they move the cows now that Jacob's barn is gone?" Simeon said to the water striders.

Simeon still felt the shrivel of flesh on his arms as he thought of what the owners of the voices, the *Blitzkafer,* could do, but at least they had faces now.

Things had definitely changed because he'd jumped on the fireman. He pictured *Daat*'s shocked face. Maybe *Daat* had thought that he was angry because of Lena A and had just taken it out on someone.

Nay, Simeon thought. *Daat* wouldn't think that. If it were Jonas, he might. Jonas had jumped Sylvan more than once. But Simeon hadn't taken his anger out on anyone before.

Simeon knew he should tell someone about the firemen in his dad's company. But what if they didn't believe him? Firemen starting a fire? Simeon could hardly believe it himself.

And then there was the cigarette. He'd probably have to tell about the cigarette. Would they arrest him, too? Simeon could already see the look on his father's face. His eyes would look far away, somewhere beyond Simeon, and then the lines from his nose to his chin would deepen.

Simeon yawned. He'd been up since three, and the tiredness was getting the best of his thoughts. He had dug a hole under two of the big roots, working at it over the last several years. The hole was pretty big now, almost a cave, and it was cool. Simeon went over and he curled up in it.

Simeon pictured the two firemen spraying the fire with the hoses after they'd set it. They used the same hands for bad and good. How could they? He felt the white-hot hate rising up again. Without thinking, his hands were fists again, beating, beating the fireman. Only the firemen weren't there anymore, and his hands were beating the sides of the cave. His right hand was getting scratched on roots.

He covered his face with his hands. He would have beaten those fireman until they couldn't even breathe if he'd been able to. He pulled his hands from his face and stared at them. Was he so different from the *Blitzkafer,* then?

Simeon's head ached. He laid it against the cool earth. Nothing would bring Lena A back. He cried until the harsh burn in his throat wouldn't let him cry anymore. He fell asleep.

Someone was shaking him. Simeon opened his eyes to see Sylvan standing there. He could tell by the place of the sun that it was late afternoon.

"How did you know where I was?" Simeon asked.

"I've been around this farm a lot longer than you have. Nice cave, though. Did you make it?"

"Ya," Simeon said. "Are you done with the milking?"

"Ya." Sylvan answered.

"Where did they move them now?"

"To Uncle Daniel's."

"That will be a ways to go for chores," Simeon said.

"Ya." Sylvan said. "Is there something you want to tell me?"

"Why?"

"The questions in the barn. And I found that my cigarettes were gone."

Simeon hadn't thought about Sylvan looking for his cigarettes.

"You need to talk, Simeon."

"*Ya.* But it's not what you think, Sylvan." Simeon's words rushed out. "I didn't start the fire, but I might have helped it."

Sylvan looked out at the creek. Simeon took a long breath. "I did go out to the barn on the night of the fire. It was to check on Dreamer. And then I got to thinking, what harm would it do to smoke one cigarette? I'd be doing it someday. I'd start sooner."

Sylvan grinned. "I did the same thing, only I smoked one of Seth's." Seth was Uncle Daniel's oldest son.

"I'd just got the cigarette lit when I heard noises in the other barn. I figured it was just the horses getting used to Dreamer. I went around to check, and a bright light flashed in my eyes. I couldn't see anything. I dropped the cigarette, and I can't remember if I stomped it out." Simeon stopped and frowned.

"Then what?"

"Someone said, 'Out for a smoke?' Then he laughed and said, 'Well, you better forget that anyone was here, because if you don't, we'll be back here, and we'll burn your house down.' And then another voice said, 'Don't breathe a word to anyone. Ever. You got that?'"

Sylvan whistled. "I would have been scared witless."

"Then I realized that the sound I'd heard earlier was a crackling, a burning sound. They'd set a fire in the barn. Up in the haymow. And then Little Elam came running out of the house. I think he was looking for me."

Simeon was quiet for a minute or two, and then Sylvan said, "And since then, you've been afraid they would set our house on fire?"

"Yes. And then everything would be worse. Little Elam, all of us."

"That explains a lot, but why did you jump on those fireman who were putting out the fire? They were just trying to help," Sylvan said.

"No, they weren't," Simeon answered.

"What?"

"I heard their voices. They were the ones who set the fire in our barn. It was the firemen. The new ones in *Daat's* company. I hadn't seen them before."

"The firemen? That doesn't make sense."

Simeon jumped up. "I'm telling the truth, Sylvan."

Sylvan's eyes crinkled at the corners, and then his mouth opened wide. He started laughing.

Simeon stared at him. His breath was coming in shallow jags. He didn't see anything funny.

Sylvan gasped long enough to say, "I do, believe you, Simeon." Then he sat on the ground. "You wouldn't have pounded those firemen otherwise. You've never even hurt a grasshopper in your whole life."

Simeon didn't want to laugh, but he couldn't help it. He sat down and laughed, too. They both laughed until they simply couldn't anymore.

"What do I do now?" Simeon asked.

"That's up to you."

"I was thinking about it before I fell asleep," Simeon said. Sylvan picked a blade of grass and chewed on the end of it while Simeon talked.

"All I could think about before was that I was trying to save our family by not saying anything. I didn't want us to be hurt anymore. But after this fire, I know I can't save anyone by myself. They might start another fire."

"I think you're right," Sylvan said.

"I think I'll tell *Daat.*"

Sylvan whistled. "That will be hard."

"I'll have to tell him about the cigarette," Simeon said.

"They were my cigarettes, and *Daat* knows I've been smoking them. I'll go with you," Sylvan said. Simeon liked the sound of those words: I'll go with you.

"But what if the fire marshal can't catch them? Don't the fire police have to prove things? What if the firemen say I started things with my cigarette?"

"The fire police know that you didn't start any other fires. You couldn't have gotten around. If you say that you heard their voices, the fire police will have to check it out."

"But what if the firebugs come after our house in the meantime? What if they find out that I told the fire marshal?"

"Then I guess we'll all take turns watching our house. There are a lot of us, and only two of them. During milking today, *Daat* said that lots of farmers are sleeping in their barns tonight."

As they walked, Simeon could see a tight line of blue-black clouds massed behind the farmhouse. The front stretched along the whole horizon. Sylvan's shirt had deep wet rings under his arms, and Simeon could feel the sweat trickling down his back. Maybe this storm would break the heat. When they got to the small barn, a group of cows was huddled together outside it with their rumps pointed toward the storm clouds.

"Simeon, I wouldn't worry about the cigarette. They'd already started the fire. By the time that cigarette lit anything, if it did, that barn was blazing."

Simeon hoped so, but he wondered if the cigarette had added even a spark. When they were almost back to the house, Sylvan said, "I'm sorry about Lena A."

Simeon just nodded. He was afraid he would cry if he said anything. Then he squared his shoulders. *"Daat,"* he called.

Chapter 14

Daat came walking out of the house. He opened his mouth to say something, but when he saw Simeon's face, he closed it.

"*Daat,* I have to tell you about the night of the fire," Simeon said.

"Let's go sit down, Simeon." They walked to the front porch, and *Daat* sat on the porch swing while Simeon climbed into a metal chair. Sylvan sat down next to him.

Simeon told his father about the night of the fire. He left nothing out. Not even the cigarettes. Simeon ended his story by saying, "I'm sorry for the smoking, *Daat.*"

Daat hadn't said anything the whole time. He didn't ask questions, as Sylvan had. He just listened and rocked. At times he stroked his beard.

"That took a lot of courage, Son," *Daat* said.

"But—" Simeon dropped his head and weaved his fingers in and out of each other. "But I was afraid."

"Seeing deep into a person can be a frightening thing. Especially when we see what we are capable of. You saw your own wrong, and that is good, Simeon. I forgive you for smoking that cigarette. Now you must let it go."

Simeon nodded.

"And I don't think you will want to smoke again," *Daat* said. A tiny smile was curving the edges of his lips.

Simeon smiled and nodded again.

"But what you saw in the others is very frightening, setting fires and threatening people." *Daat* stopped and shook his head, "We can't make them change, but we can pray for them. This is why we trust in God. In the meantime, there is *Arbeite* and *Hofe*—work and hope. We do what we can."

"Do you think they hate Amish, *Daat*?" Simeon asked.

"No, I worked with them. I think they just love fires, Simeon."

Simeon was still. "I can see that this has weighed heavy on you," *Daat* said. "It was too much for you to carry alone, Simeon. I know you were trying to care for us all, but that is too big a job for one person. Burdens are made to be shared by the community. This is our way."

Daat stood up. "Go inside and eat. You must be hungry. I will talk to the fire marshal."

That night, when Simeon went to bed, he fell fast asleep. A lightning crack filled the window, and Simeon and Little Elam both sat up. Little Elam was trembling. Simeon wrapped his arms around him and began to count: *"Eens, zwee, drei, vier, fifm,"* until a low thunder rumble stopped his voice. "See? It is a long way away."

Little Elam's body relaxed in Simeon's arms. "I wasn't in the fire, Little Elam," Simeon said. "I was outside by the barn, but I wasn't in the fire, and I'm here with you now."

They listened to the rain as it pinged on the tin roof of the back porch. "Hear the rain, Little Elam? It is a good sound." And the two brothers fell asleep.

Chapter 15

Simeon woke up earlier than usual. He listened to the sound of the chickadee and the slurred whistle of a cardinal. He realized that these were the same sounds he'd heard the morning of Lena A's calving. It seemed so long ago. Simeon held his breath, but he didn't hear anything besides the birds. He let the stillness fill him.

Later that morning, before breakfast, Simeon and Little Elam were in the small barn when *Daat* walked in. Little Elam was done feeding the calves, and he'd come in to help Simeon. The barn was crowded with the horses, dry cows, and heifers. "The barn rebuilding begins today, Simeon. That is good news, *ya*?"

Little Elam nodded and Simeon said, *"Ya."*

Daat's face stretched into a smile. His hands tensed and untensed. He can't wait to get the hammer in his hand, Simeon thought.

Men arrived early. The Amish man in charge of the project arrived, and he got the crews going. Simeon was determined to strap on a tool belt and get up there hammering with the men, but instead the contractor pointed to him. Simeon ran over. "I need you to run around for me giving my orders to everyone."

Simeon knew this was an important job. "*Ya,* sure," he said. Simeon waved at his uncle Daniel when he arrived, but they didn't have much of a chance to talk.

Simeon watched the men pouring the concrete for the foundation. The hauling of beams and the hammering and sawing went on all around him. When he saw the women setting up the long tables, he realized that he was hungry. Simeon watched as the women piled coleslaw, applesauce, red beets, chow-chow, buttered noodles, and mashed potatoes on the table. His *Maam* carried out steaming bowls of brown gravy with ham. Other women carried out the pies and puddings. He turned away and saw Little Elam running toward the small barn with his cousin Sam, Uncle Daniel's youngest son. Little Elam looks like himself again, Simeon thought.

After lunch, there was more pounding, lifting, and cutting. In midafternoon, Simeon watched as the remaining two walls were hoisted into place. It was a sight, all those men pushing and working together.

That night after supper, Simeon and *Daat* stood outside and looked at the new barn together. Simeon breathed deeply, smelling all the fresh-cut wood. He loved that smell and the way it pushed away the smell of burn.

After evening chores, *Daat* and Simeon went to Jacob's. They walked out to the pasture. Some of the horses were rolling around. Simeon laughed as he watched them, but he stopped when he realized that he didn't see Dreamer.

"Where's Dreamer?" he asked *Daat*.

"She's in the farthest pasture. By herself. She won't come in since the fire. No one has been able to get near her, but I thought maybe you could, Simeon. She knows your touch."

Yes, thought Simeon. He walked on alone. He stopped a long way from the horse. He moved forward little by little. He let the stillness of the night settle inside him. He wanted Dreamer to know the stillness, too.

He walked forward a few steps. He watched Dreamer's eye. The horse didn't move. Simeon took a few more steps. He put out his hand. He did not touch the big horse, but just stood there.

He leaned forward. His hand now touched the horse's side. He felt the tremor go through his arm. The big horse didn't move. Simeon stepped closer. He put his other hand on Dreamer. He began to whisper. "Tomorrow, tomorrow, Dreamer, I will be back. Stay in the stillness."

Simeon slowly backed away from the big horse with his hands stretched out. After twenty feet or so, he stopped and stared at his hands, but instead of his own, he saw the vet's hands, firm, strong, and gentle. This is what I am made to do, he thought. It is a gift from God. I will use my hands for healing animals. He turned and walked back toward *Daat.*

"What you think of that Dreamer?" *Daat* asked.

"She is a fine horse. She will work again. You will see," Simeon said.

"*Ya,* I knew I could trust you with her," *Daat* said.

Simeon felt some of the soreness in his chest ease out with *Daat*'s words. The soreness had lodged there between his ribs since his last look at Lena A.

"You picked a good one," *Daat* agreed. "But then, you have a way with animals."

Simeon didn't say anything. He looked up at the stars. Someday, I will be a vet, he thought.

"Simeon," *Daat* said as they turned and walked toward Jacob's house. He put his hand on Simeon's shoulder. "Dreamer is yours. She will go with you when you leave home."

Simeon's mouth was full of his tongue. "*Danki*—thanks," was all he could say.

When they got home, Little Elam ran around the new barn. He pulled Simeon toward the front yard. "I have a jar, Simeon. Let's catch the *Blitzkafer.*"

GLOSSARY OF *DEITSCH* (PENNSYLVANIA GERMAN) TERMS

Please note that there is no one standard spelling reference source for *Deitsch* words; spellings may vary according to the source. Also please note that as in German, nouns are usually capitalized.

Guide to Pronunciation:

a before any consonant except *h* = *a* as in *what*
a before *h* = *aw* as in *paw*
aa = *aw* as in *paw*
au = *ow* as in *how*
ei = *i* as in *like*
i before any consonant except *h* = *i* as in *sip*
i before *h* = *ee* as in *bee*
ie = *ee* as in *bee*
e = *e* as in *let* (*e* is pronounced at the end of words)
o = *oa* as in *coat*
oi = *oy* as in *toy*
u before most consonants = *oo* as in *soon*
u before a doubled consonant = *oo* as in *good*

Most consonants are pronounced as they are in English. Certain consonants follow a German pronunciation: *v* = *f* (as in *father*); *z* = *ts* (as in *bats*). Note that *w* is *w,* as in the English word *weather,* rather than *v,* as in German.

ach a common *Deitsch* expression similar to "oh"

Arbeite work

Blitzkafer fireflies; also in this story, firebugs (those who start fires)

Daat father

Danki thanks

darichnanner confused

Deitsch the Pennsylvania Dutch people; also their language

Demut humility

Der Herr gibt und der Herr nimmt a proverb: "the Lord giveth and the Lord taketh"

Dunnerwetter thunder weather

drei three

Englisch English-speaking Americans

eens one

fifm five

Geb acht Watch out

Gott God

Grossdawdi grandfather

Grossmudder grandmother

gut good

Gut Marye good morning

Hochmut pride

Hofe hope

Maam mother

Mache shnell hurry

Net so hatt not so hard

nunnergebrennt burnt down

nay no

Ottning the ways of the church

Rumspringa literally, "running around"; a period of time during which teenagers are allowed to experiment with worldly practices before deciding to recommit to the Amish way of life

Vas geh? Who's there?

vier four

Wo bist du? Where are you?

ya yes

zwee two

OTHER TERMS

the Aid The Amish Aid Fire and Storm Insurance Company is a Lancaster County Amish group that uses funds to help members who are victims of disaster. Many Old Order Amish believe that commercial insurance and many government programs aren't needed when the church follows the command in the Bible to "bear one another's burdens."

broadfall a style of trousers. Amish broadfall pants are black with no outside or hip pockets; they fasten with buttons and are usually held up by suspenders.

scrapple a cornmeal pudding in which the cornmeal, and perhaps a little buckwheat, is simmered with pork scraps and trimmings, then cooled and hardened into a loaf

For a reader's guide to *Simeon's Fire,* please visit www.candlewick.com.

ACKNOWLEDGMENTS

This book is a work of community. Thanks to all of you in Lancaster County who have opened your hearts and homes to us over the last twenty years. I'll do my best to thank you individually, but forgive me if I miss someone.

Thanks:
To Lloyd Miller for help with the firefighting information.
To the Witmer Fire Company for allowing me to work at the Ox Roast.

To the large animal vets who generously shared their expertise and stories over the years: Larry Kennel, Allen and Pamela Rushmer, and Bob Stoltzfus. Special thanks to the Rushmers and Bob, who invited me to go with them and "observe" what they do. I will never forget the sights and smells! Special, special thanks to Bob for reviewing the manuscript and sending me good reference material.

To the Lancaster County Library, especially Karen Haglar, periodicals clerk, who helped with newspaper research.

To the Lancaster Literary Guild for your support. Thanks, Betsy.

To Sam and Katie Lapp for connecting me with folks.

To the following farmers: the Bushong family, the Snyder family, and the Daniel Zook family, who talked while doing a whole lot of chores!

To those who shared their stories: Jake and Anna Esh, Elmer and Katie Stoltzfus, Tim and Debora Kurtz, and Gloria Spangler.

To Ray Reitz, who patiently explained the intricacies of haying, harvesting, and weather eyes.

To Kathy and Irvin Peifer for the use of Garden Gate to finish the first draft.

To the members of The Door, ACTS Covenant Fellowship, Teaching the Word Ministries, my intercessor list, and the women's prayer group that meets on Wednesdays. Your prayer support is invaluable.

To Jacob Stoltzfus and my other reader. Thanks for looking for the details.

To Karen Lotz for her affirmation and editing of this book, and to Kate Fletcher, who has done a lot of work on it.

To Lisa Bair for her encouragement to keep on writing no matter what.

To all my family, who believe in me and don't ask, "Why in the world are you writing about that?" no matter what new topic I choose.